"WHAT DO YOU WANT?"
SNAPPED HOOK LARSEN,
THE OUTLAW BOSS.

Pat nodded briefly. "I can explain in mighty few words, Larsen. We came here in hopes of hiring some of these boys."

"*You* want to hire men—what for?" he rapped out.

Introducing himself and Sam, Pat explained coolly about the horse drive to Texas.

Aware of some interested rumblings among his men, Hook roared at them, "Shut up! I'm the boss here—and I won't have no horse-driving shenanigans! Okay, boys, grab these trouble-makers and toss them—"

Turning roughly to wave an arm toward Pat and Sam, he abruptly broke off, noting with jarring surprise that Pat's Colt was out of the holster and trained squarely on his midriff. . . .

Trail Through Tascosa

A POWDER VALLEY WESTERN

by Peter Field

A KANGAROO BOOK
PUBLISHED BY POCKET BOOKS NEW YORK

TRAIL THROUGH TASCOSA

Jefferson House edition published 1963

POCKET BOOK edition published February, 1977

This POCKET BOOK edition includes every word contained in
the original, higher-priced edition. It is printed from brand-
new plates made from completely reset, clear, easy-to-read type.
POCKET BOOK editions are published by
POCKET BOOKS,
a division of Simon & Schuster, Inc.,
A GULF+WESTERN COMPANY
630 Fifth Avenue,
New York, N.Y. 10020.
Trademarks registered in the United States
and other countries.

ISBN: 0-671-80905-9.

Cover illustration by John Leone.

Printed in the U.S.A.

Trail
Through
Tascosa

1

A TALL and lithe young stranger stepped briskly from the Bar ES ranch cabin as Pat Stevens drew rein in the yard. Perhaps twenty, he wore a belted Colt .45 on his left hip. The early afternoon sun filtering through the ancient cottonwoods touched his chestnut hair with gold and there was a faint air of intolerant authority about the set of his head. "What you want?" he asked Stevens brusquely.

Pat paused to examine the young puncher—he had never set eyes on him before. "I expected to find Ezra and Sam here," he allowed mildly. "Who are you?"

"No matter." The words were even more curtly clipped. "Sorry, but the boys are pretty busy just now. If you're looking for saddle stock to buy," the young fellow went on officiously, "you're too late."

At least double the speaker's age, broad-shouldered and lean of hip, Stevens tipped the scales at close to two hundred, shading the other by a good fifty pounds. Easing his seat in the saddle, he was more amused than anything else. But the shrewd gray eyes in his bronzed face remained gravely impersonal.

"I'd just as soon let Sam tell me that," he said. "Just hired on here, did you? What do you call yourself?"

"Polk Burnett is the name. And never mind the chatter! You can take my word for it that the boys don't want to be bothered. . . . Some other time, mister," he suggested significantly.

But Pat ignored this brash attempt to send him packing. He could hear the sounds of stamping horses and excited yelling drifting faintly from the direction of the big south pasture. "That's them now, I expect—" With no intention of leaving without having seen his crusty old friends, who had run the little horse ranch in the lower end of Powder Valley for a number of years now, he turned that way.

"Hold on, you!" Burnett started forward. "Nobody's allowed out there, do you hear? That goes for everybody—so do as I say and come back later!"

Pat's return was a cool stare which needed no words and halted young Burnett in his tracks; he had already pushed his horse past the corner of the cabin. Glancing beyond, he saw the churning mass of roans in the pasture and made out the figures of his friends flitting about through the clouds of dust.

As Pat moved forward purposefully, Polk Burnett dashed back into the cabin. Emerging from the rear, he swung up on his waiting horse and came jogging stubbornly after. He was prudent enough to keep his distance, but if his grim expression meant anything it spelled trouble for Stevens.

Nearing the pasture gate, Pat was struck by the fact that the partners had gathered a magnificent roan herd of unprecedented size and royal bearing. Surely something unusual was afoot. He let himself carefully through the gate, paying no heed whatever to the vociferous objections from young Polk which rose above the rush and thunder of hoofs.

Sam Sloan, a stout, beefy individual clad in frayed and straining bib overalls, spotted him and came jogging forward with nonchalant importance, his legs jutting grotesquely over the bulging sides of his mount. "Take your look at this bunch of roan hides, boy," he crowed cheerfully.

"Why all the mystery, Sam?" Pat barked with pretended severity.

Sloan's blue-bristled moonface showed his perplexed astonishment. "Huh?" His tone was blank. "What's mysterious about a bunch of horses as big as this one?" he demanded tartly.

Pat waved backward toward the scowling puncher.

"I can't figure that one myself. But if I'd listened to your watchdog here, I'd never have had a look."

"Shucks." Eying Pat's grave face and Burnett's sheepish one, Sloan caught on fast. "Polk had his orders to keep the idle drifters out of here. You'll admit yourself, Stevens, at first glance anybody would be justified in being suspicious of your looks!"

"Oh, go jump in the wash." The bond between these old cronies was so close that anything resembling politeness was sure to be met with derision. "What are you and Ez up to, anyway?"

"Big sale coming up, boy." Sam showed his snaggle teeth in an expansive grin. "The buyer is due today to look this stuff over. Burnett knew you couldn't be him."

"Oh?" Pat's tone chilled. "Just how does he know, may I ask?"

"You don't wear no uniform, for one thing." Sam chucked triumphantly. "And for another, Stevens, I don't think you're ready to offer as much as we expect to get for these high-grade horses."

Little as it showed in his actions or his ambitious talk of plans, Sam Sloan was crowding sixty, like his lanky, one-eyed partner Ezra. A good twenty years younger, in the robust prime of life, Stevens had been often called upon in years past to yank the battered pair of hardshells out of assorted fiascoes. Repeatedly he had saved them from the consequences of their own folly; and if his sole reward was scant thanks for his effort, it did not prevent him from keeping a wary eye on their reckless affairs.

"A uniform, you say?" Pat's glance sharpened. "You mean the army is considering this stuff?"

"That's exactly what I mean." Sam's confidence was boundless. "Ez agreed to let me do the dickering for once. Stick around, young fellow, and watch what happens. Major Couch promised to be here early this afternoon. We're expecting him to show up any minute. . . . Keep an eye peeled there at the house, Burnett!" He waved the young puncher that way. "We don't want to miss connections, or keep the major waiting."

Polk turned away, and a moment later Ezra pushed close around the edge of the restless, milling herd. Sam's partner was lean as a slat; the black flatbrim he wore cocked forward over his hawklike face shadowed a black patch over the empty socket of one eye, lost in a fight years back. "Howdy there, Stevens," he called out gruffly. "I see you're flocking around the honey, same as the rest of the flies!"

"This is the finest bunch of roans I ever saw on the Bar ES, Ez," Pat gave back frankly. "Lots of them, too. I didn't realize you had so much good stock. I'm glad of it for you two."

Ez shook his grizzled head. "No soft soap, now," he retorted good-humoredly. "We can't part with a head of this stuff, as it happens—even to you."

Pat's eyes twinkled. No thought of dickering for a few choice animals had entered his head, but he was not above needling the tough old rawhide. "Got every head earmarked for the army, have you?" he tossed back lightly. "I seem to recall another horse deal the army was interested in—"

He was referring to a case not too long ago which had nearly ended in disaster for the craggy partners as well as himself. At the time Ezra had made remarks about the army which he preferred not to remember at present.

"Go ahead—bring up that old chestnut again!" Ezra's leathery visage turned red. "This is a different deal altogether, and you know it—"

"Sure, sure. I understand. It's always different, Ez." Stevens pretended to pacify him, all the while adding fuel to the fire.

He was gathering his forces for a devastating blast when Sloan, who had been gazing toward the ranch house, barked, "Lay off it, you two! This must be Major Couch coming now." He nodded his bullet head, his black pupils sharpening. "Can the clowning and keep out from underfoot while I make short work of this deal."

They saw young Burnett riding toward them accompanied by an elderly, stern-faced man clad in officer's garb. "Boys, this here is Major Couch from Matagorda," the puncher called out as they drew near.

Sloan pushed his way forward. "How do, Major. I'm Sloan—and that's my partner Ezra yonder," he opened up, with an offhand casualness that made Ez mutter under his breath. "I suppose you've come to check on our horses—"

Jubal Couch advanced to meet him and shook hands punctiliously. "That's right, Sloan. Glad to see you've got the animals gathered where I won't have to waste time. This *is* the herd you're offering for sale?" he broke off, clipping the words carefully.

Sam waved expansively toward the frisky roans. "That's right. There they are, Major. You'll hunt far and wide for a finer bunch of horseflesh, if I do say it myself." He chuckled at his own pleasantry.

Couch did not so much as crack a smile. All business, he at once set about examining the roans in detail. Critical to the point of finicking, he called attention to one extremely minor defect after another until Ezra turned away in disgust, reining over to join Stevens a little apart.

"Either he aims to beat Sam down or he just ain't interested, picking faults all over the place like that," he growled gloomily.

Pat did not think so. "He's interested all right or he wouldn't give a whoop," he pointed out. "At a snap judgment, I'd say the army is really out for horses."

Ez grudgingly nodded. "He wrote us they're wanted for cavalry remount," he admitted. "But right now it sounds like they want the stuff for nothing. . . . Listen to that Sam agree with every complaint!"

Sloan was working closely with the officer, putting in a word where he could but making no demur to Couch's criticisms. At one point the major wanted a horse roped and thrown, so that he could examine mouth and hoofs. Ez and Pat took a hand, and it was not lost on the officer that every one of these magnificent roans packed fire and force under its sleek hide; still he had a routine to follow. It would have been impossible to tell from his inscrutable face what his conclusions might be. Not until he and Sloan had pretty well combed the entire herd did the man desist. From his practiced glance alone, Stevens guessed the major knew horses and was not fooled for a minute about what he might be getting.

Couch and Sam came riding back at length, gravely discussing the general merits of the herd. By this time Sam was talking with his hands. "You won't find better stuff for saddle stock, Major," he averred. "Specially for use in desert country—if that's your aim. These broncs can live on air and cactus, and get fat."

Couch's cautious agreement was dry. "We can use these horses," he admitted. "It all hangs on whether we strike a satisfactory agreement or not."

Sam paused. He was too smart to set any asking price. He would have named a figure of fifty or sixty dollars a head, straight through, had he dared; but you never knew about the army. A difference of a dollar or two might kill a promising deal—or it might not.

"So what's your offer, Major?" he asked. "Ez and me aren't too hard to please. But we know what we've got here too."

Couch glanced again over the fiery roans. "The best I'm empowered to offer is eighty a head," he clipped off with decision.

Sam's eyes started to bug out before he caught himself. Ezra sucked in a deep breath, almost swept away by the fantastic sum this would add up to for the whole herd. Even Pat was amazed by the generosity of the offer.

"Eighty a head, straight through, did you say?" Sam echoed slowly, gazing at the officer as if expecting he had made a mistake.

Couch's nod was curt. "That'll have to be a final offer, Sloan—for a count as close to three hundred head as you can make it. With prompt payment guaranteed on delivery at Matagorda, Texas."

Hearing that name again, Stevens abruptly comprehended the reason for such a generous price. He ran a hand across his lean jaw, wiping off a smile. Sam seemed to smell a rat too, for he delayed, frowning.

"Texas, Major?" He grunted. "I don't know about making delivery that far away. . . . Why not knock say five dollars off the price and accept range delivery? That way your boys can be working with the horses while they're driving them," he offered weakly.

Couch's reaction was decidedly negative. "You seem not to have heard we're on the verge of a war with Mexico, Sloan. I simply can't spare a cavalry detail right now—and I'll just add that the offer for these roans here on the Bar ES would have to be forty dollars. Only I'm not interested."

Pat read how shrewd the major was in dangling a juicy price first, and only afterward tacking on his inexorable conditions. Even Ezra was thrown into a quandary—he made furtive gestures toward Sam.

"Three hundred head is a lot of horses." Sam was manfully stalling. "I don't know just how soon we can round up a crew and get started. There might be delays on the trail too—"

"Make up your mind, man," barked Couch in his best military manner. "Wars don't wait! I haven't time for you to blow hot and cold. I need those horses at once, and if I can't have them on my terms I'll be forced to look elsewhere. What'll it be?" Shoulders thrown back, he awaited the outcome of his ultimatum.

Ezra's chagrin at his partner's stubborn stand exploded in a violent snort. "Say yes, you nitwit!" he hurled at Sam. "Before I send you out to peddle those broncs one at a time!"

Never noted for exerting undue control over what they said to each other, at any other time Sloan would have indulged in a vituperative combat with his lanky partner on the spot. Under these circumstances, however, he shrugged his thick shoulders and glanced at the officer in droll resignation.

"That's what I'm up against, Major," he said. "Looks like I'm obliged to take up your officer, or I'll never hear the end of it!"

Endlessly entertained by the bickering of this crotchety pair, Stevens allowed his glance to stray to Major Couch's face in what amounted to a wink. The officer grunted, his mouth stern as ever.

"Very well. . . . This strikes me as highly irregular," he grumbled slightingly, "but I'll draw up an agreement." Producing paper and traveling pen, he went to work on his saddle-horn, his thin lips moving. He handed the result across to Sloan. "You're both expected to sign that as partners."

Sam laboriously did as he was told, then he handed the paper and pen to Ezra. Scowling, Ez made a sprawling cross on the spot indicated. Sam exchanged a surprised look with Pat, but neither of them said anything.

"I suppose that's your promise to pay on delivery of this stock at Matagorda," Sam said, handing the document to Couch and starting to stuff the copy in his pocket without looking at it.

"By no means." The major caught him up tartly. "It's *your* agreement to deliver the horses as contracted herein. In case you've forgotten, you're dealing with the United States Government, my man. Just see that you carry out your commitment and there'll be no difficulty whatever."

Crestfallen over his mistake, Sam looked ready to throw the paper away in exasperation. But there was no way out, the executed agreement having disappeared beyond recall into the officer's pocket.

"That completes our business, I believe." Looking now like the cat that swallowed the canary, Couch gathered up his reins. "I'll meet you in Matagorda within one month, gentlemen—and good luck." Without more ado he turned briskly away, plainly intent on wasting no more time here.

Stunned by the celerity of it all, the partners gazed after his departing back, and it was Polk Burnett who hastily let the major out at the pasture gate.

Waiting barely until he was beyond earshot, Sam whirled angrily toward his lean-jawed partner. "What's this about making your X on that paper? You can write your name—if not much else!" he flared. "Was it your idea to leave me holding the bag on that contract, or what?"

Ezra's single slitted pupil was icy. "Wanted to make this deal, didn't you?" he growled defensively. "Ain't no satisfying some people—"

Sam came back with a scorching retort, and there would have been a hot argument on the spot but for Pat's laugh. Sam whirled, favoring him with a sour look. "What would that be about, Stevens?" he barked.

Pat's grin widened. "You two sure bit on a loaded plug that time. . . . Eighty dollars a head, is it?" he drawled. "Just remember that three hundred head of these roans means cleaning your range! And delivery at Matagorda—" he drove the point home with cruel frankness—"spells a tough drive clear down across the Panhandle through the worst outlaw country in Texas. You'll never make it!"

2

FOLLOWING PAT'S DERISIVE prediction, Ezra rasped accusingly at his partner, "In an awful sweat to sign that crazy agreement with the army, weren't you?"

"Who was it making all those secret motions to

sign up while I was thinking it over?" Sam did not conceal his angry exasperation. "And furthermore, I got just one question to ask you, beanpole. *Did* you—or didn't you—sign that agreement yourself, to the best of your ability anyhow?"

Ez could not deny that he had made his X before witnesses. He shrugged contemptuously. "Went along with the business to back you up. You know what this means, of course. In your hustle to grab at a fat price you threw away what little capital we got!"

Sam's laugh was bitter. "You knew all that—so you helped me throw it away. Is that what you're squawking about?" He had more to say; his remarks were blistering. Ezra took him up heatedly, and for some minutes they lashed out at each other.

Returning while they were still at it, Polk Burnett looked from one to the other with slowly widening eyes. He must have thought this partnership on the verge of dissolution. But Stevens knew better. Masking his amusement, he waited until he could get a word in.

"You make a hot combination, I'll grant that," he interjected calmly at the first opening. "But all this doesn't solve your problem—if either one of you noticed!"

They whirled on him in unison. "Mighty superior, ain't you, Stevens?" snarled Ez. "Just what would *you* do in our situation?"

Pat shrugged lazily. "What could anyone do? I'd make delivery, of course, before the army commandeers this stock at their own price."

"Oh, you would. And just how?" barked Sam, watching him narrowly.

"Well, in your boots," Pat said, "I suppose I'd try to hire me a bunch of owlhoots to make that drive. They know their own kind best."

"Sure. So simple there's nothing to it!" Sam snorted. "And where would you say we could pick up a handful of assorted outlaws around here at a moment's notice?"

"That's right." Ezra took up Sam's argument. "Explain to us why owlhoots should work hard for small pay, Stevens, when they can just as easily steal their own horses."

"You asked what I'd do, and I told you. . . . You can try anyway, can't you?" Pat urged coolly.

"Let's see. Did you mention where?" pressed Sam.

"Well, you heard the same as I did that the Kansas Pacific hired an army of owlhoots and rough characters this spring," Pat began.

It was true. Each spring saw the renewal of the perennial railroad wars in the Arkansas river canyons, where a scarcity of practicable right-of-way gave rise to bitter rivalry between the big lines. Just now the K.P. was locked in a death struggle with the Santa Fe. Outlaws and gunmen could always count on big pay during the fierce clashes arising over the disputed mountain passages.

"We can't pay those cutthroats what the railroads are offering," objected Ez.

"That's true." Pat nodded. "But maybe you wouldn't have to. I understand the Santa Fe rounded up a battalion of federal marshals this year, Ez. They must be making it rough for those outlaws; and in spite of the big pay a lot of them are probably ready to call it quits."

Ez glanced up hopefully at this. But the possibility seemed far-fetched, and his face fell. "That's a hundred to one chance," he grumbled.

Stevens was ready for him. "What kind of a chance would you say you have of driving across the Panhandle on your own?" he countered flatly.

Ez looked blankly at his partner, and they exchanged scowls. "We can try it on, I suppose," allowed Sam uneasily. Then he whirled on Pat. "But this is your hare-brained scheme, remember! Are you coming with me, Stevens?" He was talking fast now. "Ez and Polk can watch the horses—"

"I expect I can go along in a pinch." Although Pat did not sound enthusiastic, he would not have missed the adventure for the world. "Someone will have to keep you out of trouble, and I'm usually the goat."

His jibe was passed over in Ezra's disgruntlement at being left out. "You already talked youself into one jackpot," he hurled at Sam sourly. "Just be sure you don't promise to hand over the roans to them owlhoots for their pay!"

Sam's laugh was caustic. "I won't—if you'll undertake not to get into a poker game with 'em," he retorted.

"Come on, come on." Pat pretended impatience. "If we've got to pick up some hands, Sloan, let's get about it."

"Well, I got to get me a fresh horse." Sam sounded injured. "Shake it up here, Ez, and help me—"

Ezra gave him a withering look, and it was young Polk who lent a hand, adeptly snaring the stalwart roan Sam indicated and leading it forward. The one-eyed man stolidly watched as they quickly transferred the saddle. "I suppose I can look forward to your whooping it back here with a parcel of owlhoots flogging your tail," he growled. "Does it make any difference how many hands we can use, or will you weed 'em out with a six gun?"

In spite of himself, Pat gave an amused chuckle. "You're right, Ez," he agreed. "We ought to plan what we're doing right from the start." He paused. "Six hands could ordinarily drive this number of broomtails. But for these salty army broncs—and going all that way to the Texas coast—I'd suggest at least eight men."

He waited, glancing at the partners for comment. For ten minutes they soberly discussed the practical details with an absence of levity or animosity that even further surprised Polk Burnett. The rough-edged give and take of these three old friends, and their ability to get down to brass tacks at need, was a revelation to the young puncher. Burnett had never met men just like them, and now, considering the risky project they were about to take on as casually as they treated one another, his opinion of their courage soared. But he still thought the scheme as foolish as anything he had ever heard.

With their plans straightened out at length, Pat said, "We'll get on over to the Lazy Mare right off, Sam. I want to leave orders with Johnson. And we can get an early start in the morning."

"I'll look for you back in three days," Ezra called gruffly as the pair started off. "If you're not here by then I'll send a posse."

"Make it a big one," Stevens threw over his shoulder. "Because we'll be where the little ones won't count."

It was roughly a two-hour ride to Pat's prosperous cattle ranch north of Dutch Springs. From their talk along the trail, it could not have been surmised that either was concerned over the outcome of their adventure. Pat asked about young Burnett, and was told he had been hired a couple of days before while riding the grub-line.

"He's a good worker," vouchsafed Sam. "If he seems young, that's nothing a little seasoning won't cure."

Pat agreed. "Having him along on the drive will help to take the curse off these hard-boiled nubbins you'll be forced to hire."

They reached the Lazy Mare at dusk, and after supper Stevens spent an hour with his foreman Zeke Johnson. Sam passed the time in the ranch kitchen with grumpy old Crusty Hodge, whom Sloan had taken the trouble to cultivate in the past and whose opinion of him in consequence was high.

Crusty had breakfast waiting for them an hour before dawn the following morning, and daylight found the pair well on their way north across the open range. It was an all-day ride across waste country and barren ridges.

In late afternoon the land tilted downward across the long slopes to the rugged Arkansas canyon. Beyond the tortuous river gorge the Rockies loomed skyward. The Arkansas itself ran sullenly below rough rocky walls; and it was through the narrow gorge that the railroad threaded a perilous passage, creeping along the ledges.

The peaks here were so nearly impenetrable for hundreds of miles in every direction that any means of traverse, however difficult, was at a premium. Great railroad companies, keenly aware of the riches waiting in the mining fields, fought without gloves for the possession of every available right-of-way across the lofty mountains to the Coast. Gunmen were shamelessly hired and countless murders perpetrated in the battle for mastery of the rocky canyons. The small armies, fighting for the gorges or high passes, but unable to rout each other, sometimes found themselves at a stalemate. It was such a situation which Stevens was bent on exploiting for his own purposes.

It would not be easy. The railroad points were armed camps, with the tracks between patrolled by guards. All strangers were suspect; it would be a feat to so much as locate the men they sought. After that would come the problem of persuading them to listen.

Dusk found Pat and Sam drawing near Coal Creek, a tiny Rio Grande supply point and cattle-loading station. Sloan looked down into the canyon at the tangle of shadowy corrals and a dozen roofs, where faint lights already gleamed in the bottom of the canyon. "Where'll we find these men you're looking for?" he asked, tossing a glance back at Stevens as they started down the looping trail.

Pat was unconcerned. "We'll let the next few hours tell us that," he rejoined. "They can't be far away. Just don't give the game away too fast. We'll play this by ear."

It suited Sam. "We'll grab a bait in the railroad hash-house, and maybe put up the broncs here for the night," he suggested.

The trail pitched downward steeply, forcing them to advance with care. Darkness descended into the canyon with them and the stars came out, glinting on the brawling waters of the Arkansas. Cottonwoods grew on the flats; the steel tracks of the Rio Grande line curved out of a narrow granite-walled gateway, passed through the tiny settlement and disappeared again into the rocky corridor of the river gorge beyond.

Coal Creek boasted only a single short street with a wooden station building at one end and a network of malodorous stock corrals strung along the tracks opposite; a general store, a barber shop, two saloons and what looked like a railroad boarding house lined the other side of the street. The restaurant was in one corner of the latter building, with a door opening on the street. As in most railroad towns the grimy structures were all ramshackle and unpainted, the windows dingy with coal smoke.

A silent figure moved here and there through the gloom, masculine voices sounded from the door of a bar, and the window lights dimly illuminated short stretches of the dusty street. The two friends drew rein before the hash-house, glancing about before they dismounted.

"Awful quiet around here," muttered Sam.

Pat's answer was brief. "Seems that way. We'll see."

Racking their mounts, they stepped into the eatery. A few late customers, mostly yard men or roustabouts, were having supper. Their own garb plainly marked Pat and Sam as stockmen, yet the waiter scowled in their direction and took long enough in serving them. Although Sam grumbled ominously under his breath, Stevens evinced no outward evidence of irritation.

A silence had fallen in the place at their entrance, and they said little to break it. Before they were done eating, a tall giant of a man clad in neat dark clothes stepped in from the street. There was something authoritative and baleful in his heavy manner. His head turned slowly; he glimpsed the pair sitting at the counter and deliberately moved forward. His deep voice rumbled, "Saw your horses out there. What you after here?"

Pat took a swallow of coffee, set the cup down, and turned to examine the big man. "As you say, we did reach here by saddle. And we'll ride out again the same way. Sit down, neighbor, and have some coffee," he invited him coolly.

The other digested this in silence, raking their faces with brooding eyes. Without a word he turned and moved back to the desk, where he held a muttered conversation with the clerk. Well aware he was waiting for them, Sam and Pat finished their meal without haste and got up. The heavy-faced man moved aside while they paid their bill but was close behind when they stepped outside. His harsh voice brought them to a stand still barely beyond the door.

"All right—give it a name," he rasped tightly.

Pat stepped close, eyeing the man sharply in the faint light. "You're a railroad bull, aren't you? . . . We're stock raisers, mister, lining up hands for a drive. Give us a hand in locating those K. P. owlhoots I understand are around," he proposed coolly, "and we'll take half a dozen of them off your back."

The detective weighed this inscrutably for a space, then stepped back. "You talk like a cow jockey," he allowed gruffly. "It just happens I can't help you."

Sam was incredulous. "You mean you don't know where those gun-slingers are holed up?" he demanded.

"I said I can't help you." The big fellow raised his voice. "And if you're smart, hombre, you'll pull out of the canyon fast. There ain't nothing for you here."

Sam would have argued vehemently but the other man did not wait, fading into the shadows. Sloan's snort was contemptuous. "We taking *his* advice?"

Pat did not reply directly, glancing toward the lights of a bar. "Think I'll have me a drink," he remarked.

Sam read his thought. Shoulder to shoulder they moved toward the saloon and stepped in. Despite the adobe floor it was plainly a railroaders' hangout. The bar was lit by an old-fashioned brakeman's lantern, and a shiny brass locomotive lamp hung above the cracked mirror. The dark-visaged men lining the bar and grouped about various tables, however, were a mixed lot. Grimy railroad caps with up-tilted peaks mingled with broad-brimmed range Stetsons; and some of these men must have been townsmen or drifters.

Glances were cast toward the two, who stepped to the end of the bar; but the rumbling talk and rough badinage did not break off. A noisy braggart at the other end of the bar quickly distracted attention from Pat and Sam. They got their drinks and sampled them.

Taking time to light a smoke, Stevens allowed his glance to stray over the place. Taking in the lithe, rugged figures, there seemed every likelihood that some of the men he sought might be here even now. He seemed to detect an atmosphere of tension in the room, and there was no denying this was a large collection of men for so small a town.

Sam had spotted a battered range acquaintance who accosted him from across the intervening tables. "What you doing here, Sloan?" he sang out.

"I guess nothing—when a man can't even get stock cars." Sam's shrug was whimsical. "Ain't been able to place an order for cars in the last two weeks. It's one heck of a note when a railroad is scared out by a handful of cow thieves—"

His design was deep. The statment marked him and Stevens at once as wholly disinterested in the railroad wars as such. While the Rio Grande was not ostensibly involved in the current struggle, it was vulnerable from the mere fact of its extensive operations through the rugged Rockies. The circumstance made its employees restless. A mustached off-duty conductor gave Sloan a frosty scrutiny.

"Why don't you drive your stinking cows where they're going, Buster" he inquired scathingly.

Sam was quite ready to bandy this brand of talk at a moment's notice. "Why don't you run your railroad the way it ought to be run, and let me run my business?" he retorted with gusto.

The words were scarcely out of his mouth when a husky enginehand whirled from the near-by table and slugged the rotund little man alongside the head.

3

SAM WENT BACKWARD with a crash. He could almost be said to have bounced, for he was up so quickly that Stevens could not have checked his vigorous swing at his assailant had he wanted to.

To do him full credit the fiery little rooster was good in a roughhouse fight. At the last instant he swiftly altered his aim at the railroader's guarded jaw and slammed his rocky fist into the man's unprotected stomach. Down he went in his turn, gagging for breath.

This unexpected development had an instantaneous effect on the place. Aroused yells broke out. Men rose to their feet. A trackman cursed the range men in shrill excitement, and a tall man in a soiled Stetson promptly belted him with all his strength. Others as quickly pitched into the melee, a bottle sailed across the saloon, and in a matter of seconds the place was a seething pandemonium.

The brawl plainly revealed the divided loyalties of these men. All had been waiting for the first excuse to do battle. If Pat was astonished at the suddenness of it he did not reveal his surprise, shouldering aside a gandy dancer who aimed a kick at Sam from behind.

Fortunately, the room was small enough to check a certain amount of violence. Yells echoed, brake-sticks made their appearance as if by magic, and a man or two went down. These men were quickly jammed into a struggling mass. Pat and Sam found themselves swept irresistibly against the bar, which creaked and swayed under the mounting pressure.

Sam's short legs were swept out from under him and he smashed to the earthen floor, the scant space above him filled with struggling, straining bodies. Forcing his way forward, Stevens bent over him and hoisted Sam up as far as his knees. "Make for the door," he called above the clatter and uproar in the bar, giving Sam a thrust in that direction. "If a gun goes off here it'll be bad!"

Despite his itch for combat, Sloan was inclined to agree with him. There was nothing to be gained in a free-for-all, regardless of the tangled motives at the bottom of it. Others may have felt the same, which accounted for the almost impenetrable jam blocking the exit. Seeking to work toward it, the pair were unable to get far.

"Let's go, cowpokes! We got to break this up!" a tall, black-haired range hand bawled, flailing right and left as he plowed into the seething mass. Several companions sprang to back up his effort.

Sam prudently steered in their wake, with Stevens at his heels. The group made an effective battering ram, pushing inexorably forward. Cries of pain and protest rang out, and men went down under the onslaught. There was a fierce conflict at the door. Abruptly the barrier gave way and the Powder Valley pair found themselves catapulted into the open.

As the fighting spilled out into the street, brickbats began to fly about. A missile struck Sloan's rotund corporation, fetching a muffled grunt from him. "Oof—!" Sam was not above reaching down for whatever had hit him, burning for swift retaliation, but Pat hustled him on without ceremony.

"Make for the broncs, Sam!" the lean range man barked. "There's nothing for us in this scramble—"

They ran for the waiting horses. It was a wise move. Yells of fury rang out behind them and a shot split the night. Swinging astride, they whirled away as the thud of other hoofs came to their ears from somewhere in the gloom.

"They can't be on our heels already," Sam sang out in alarm.

Pat crowded Sam's mount into a run ahead of his

own. "Don't think so," he tossed back. "Somebody else on the run too, more than likely. Make for that trail up the canyon wall, Sam!"

They raced that way, avoiding the lighted buildings. Yells rang fainter to the rear. Approaching the foot of the climbing trail, they appeared to be alone in the star-shot darkness.

Not until the loops of the trail lifted them well above the canyon floor did they slow down to save the horses. "We made it." Cocking his ear as he spoke, Sam listened to the muted uproar still drifting up to them from Coal Creek. "Do you hear broncs, Stevens—?" He broke off alertly.

Pat grunted. "Somebody climbing the trail behind us—I think."

The sounds grew plainer as they proceeded. Still Stevens did not hurry, gauging the faint crack of hoofs with a keenly attuned ear. "You aim to run into them?" Sam threw out in a tense undertone.

"That's right," was the surprising reply, "once we're close enough to the top to get away in a pinch. I want to know who that is, if I can."

Sam was game. They measured their speed, gradually allowing their followers to draw up. Near the canyon's rim the low moon cast a ghostly, slanting light across the mesquite. The ring of hoofs was louder now. Peering back, Stevens thought he could make out a trio of mounted figures.

As he and Sam lagged, the mutter of gruff voices, suddenly dying out, warned that they had been seen. The trail wound out into the open. Still the trio behind them pressed forward boldly. Pat reined discreetly out of the road as they drew near, hauling up beside Sam and waiting.

The strangers rode close, peering silently around in the pale light. The five men measured one another like strange dogs. Finally one of the hard-faced trio spoke. "You the hombre that set off that ruckus there in Coal Creek, fatty?" he tossed at Sam.

"Could be," the latter returned briefly. "Thought

for a minute I stubbed my toe on a stick of dynamite."

The remark elicited a snort of harsh mirth. "You were in luck, having us handy, in case you didn't get it, friend," one of the strangers said. "You're in the clear now—so shove off."

Sam and Pat exchanged glances at this, without response. "Well, are you going?" one of the roughs rasped.

For answer Pat waved them past. "There's the trail, boys," he invited quietly. "We'll look after ourselves."

The trio weighed this for a space. "Well—" One of them started on, the other two following at a deliberate pace. A distance apart, Pat started up the trail in their wake with Sam at his side. Watching this, the trio halted uncertainly; but when the pair behind them stopped also, they presently started on again.

Ten minutes later after mumbling inaudibly together they suddenly branched off the trail and set out across the brush at a brisk trot. Pat as promptly swung that way, mending his own gait. "You sure you know what you're up to, boy?" Sam growled, clinging to his flank.

Pat's nod was untroubled. "Sure do. I've got a hunch they're owlhoots, Sam, and their actions say the same."

His interest flaring in a twinkling, Sam was keyed up for anything that might develop. It was not long in coming. Seeing their maneuver, the trio raced ahead; but finding themselves unable to shake off the dogged pair at their heels, they stopped once more, and one of them came jogging back menacingly.

"What do you want with us?" he ripped out, confronting them at a dozen yards.

"Maybe nothing, Buster." Pat waved him away. "Said we'd take care of ourselves, didn't I?"

The range rough turned back to join his fellows, and they conferred in low-voiced colloquy. Finally the three came purposefully forward. "Let 'em have it, Josh," muttered one hardily.

"Where you going?" rasped Josh.

"I don't know. Where are you?" countered Pat coolly.

"Hell, this is a game! You playing it with them, Pierce?" burst out one of the trio.

Josh Pierce gestured briefly. "You know what to do, Alamo."

Pat noted again that Alamo was the one with a rifle slanting across his saddle-bow. He circled circumspectly, falling in behind Pat and Sam. Pierce turned his bronc.

"Okay, let's go——"

They set off, with Stevens and his stocky friend following the pair in the lead while Alamo brought up the rear. Neither of the two captives appeared disturbed by the circumstance.

"Where we heading, boys?" inquired Sam brightly.

Pierce favored him with an ominous scrutiny. "You'll find out, since you're bound to."

"Sure." Sam was almost chummy. "I just thought you could tell me."

Silence fell as they rode. The ride was long. A couple of hours passed. As they crossed a ridge Sam gazed about the range, asking himself where they were headed.

Pat had a better idea. As they thrust onward he recognized, rising to the fore, a rocky mesa of distinctive shape which stood not many miles from the busy mining camp of Florence. This had already been the scene of several bloody clashes in the railroad wars, and his pulse quickened as he noted the trail they followed, rising steadily toward the high crown of the isolated mesa.

The moon was sinking as they topped out, but there was enough diluted light by which to scan the irregular mesa top, Stevens had been right in his guess that the trio were hired owlhoots or gunmen, and that they would lead the way to the outlaw camp. The camp lay in the open with no particular attempt made to guard the trails or even post a watch. Half a dozen campfires glowed and flickered, visible at a distance of a quarter-mile. At least thirty or forty dark figures could be made out moving about the fires. Yet their own tiny party had not yet been accosted. Pat surmised these iron-nerved men were sufficiently sure of themselves to entertain no fear of attack.

The five jogged steadily on through the heaps of broken rock and low, ragged ledges tufted with brush. It was possible as they drew close to make out a rope corral holding upward of fifty or sixty horses. Others, doubtless favorites of their owners, were staked out in the brush. Noting the natural defenses of this apparently unguarded camp, the Powder Valley pair gazed keenly toward the men standing, sitting or moving about the fires. Both felt a keen curiosity about the reception they would meet here. It was from this lawless, hard-living collection of men that they hoped to recruit the drovers they needed.

Riding up to the edge of the camp, they tethered their mounts in the brush. The moon had dipped below the edge of the western peaks, and dawn was brightening the east. Most of these owlhoots, it could now be made out, were occupied with early morning chores. Some were preparing breakfast, others washing up in a hatful of water, and yet others were struggling into boots and jackets. Nearly all seemed preoccupied with their own affairs, silent in morning gloom.

Josh Pierce motioned Sam and Pat toward a campfire on the edge of the camp. Stevens at once singled out a rawboned giant sipping steaming coffee from a battered can. Beetle-browed and raw-hewn of visage, he appeared from his complete indifference to those about him to be a leader.

The arrival of Pierce's small party had caused no stir whatever. A man folding up a bedroll called out: "Howdy, Alamo," and the hard-faced giant turned to scan the new arrivals. His flinty eye passed over Josh and his companions to rest squarely on Stevens and Sam.

"What do them two want?" he snapped.

It was Pierce, leading the way toward him, who responded. "Let them answer, Larsen," he gave back loudly, putting a stress on his words. "They dogged us here."

Pat and Sam exchanged a fleeting glance. Hook Larsen was a name to conjure with in outlaw annals. Any doubt that they had located one of the main owlhoot camps was dispelled, and this was without doubt the notorious Hook himself.

"No go, Pierce. We ain't taking on any more hands," the big outlaw flung out.

"You got us wrong, Larsen. We're not looking for a job," Sam said with impudent ease.

"Okay. Spit it out." Hook lifted a menacing glance to Pat's lean face.

It seemed plain enough from his surly greeting that they were being taken for railroad spies, despite their unmistakable identity as range men. Pat nodded briefly. "I can explain in mighty few words, Larsen. We came here in hopes of hiring half a dozen of these boys."

A few owlhoots, attracted by the gruff talk, had turned or started this way to watch and listen. Others joined them, one or two at a time, until a considerable audience had collected to examine the newcomers. Larsen may have had some idea of playing up to them, for he displayed scornful incredulity.

"*You* want to hire men—what for?" he rapped out.

Introducing himself and Sam, Pat explained coolly about the horse drive to Matagorda on the Texas coast. "All your boys are expert stock handlers," he pointed out. "And we'll need the best, working down across the Panhandle and through the mountains—"

"I see." Big Hook pretended to listen closely. "And what are you paying for this—expert help, Stevens?" he asked sardonically.

Pat named a modest monthly salary, a fair enough offer for legitimate range hands. It raised a grim laugh among these hardbitten listeners. "You kidding?" a hawk-faced man jeered. "What do you think we're drawing right now, stranger?"

Pat was fully aware that his offer seemed petty

compared to their inflated stipend as hired gunmen. Yet he was prepared to meet the objection with a reasonable argument.

"These broncs we're driving are army stock," he let fall without particular emphasis. "I understand some of you boys are honing to join the cavalry— there's a war coming up against Mexico, you know. The army's gathering down there near the border. They'll probably take the hands making this delivery," he added.

"Hey, there's a notion, Larsen!" an outlaw sang out. "Quite a few of the gang's been figuring how to join up with the cavalry!"

The outlaw leader scowled. "So you want to nurse an army mule now, Skurlock?"

"I'd nurse two of 'em to git in that fight with Mexico," retorted Skurlock boldly.

"That's right! Tell the man, Chunk!" another burst out vigorously. "Guarantee us a berth in that cavalry, Stevens, and I'm all for you."

"Me too! . . . Count me in, Stevens!" the cries came, drawing Hook Larsen's bitter scorn.

Pat held up a hand, glancing coldly about. "Sorry, boys. No promises. I'm not Uncle Sam and I don't run the army. I don't doubt you'll make it in if you're serious about it—and I'll put in a word for anyone who wants to volunteer. But as I say, you're on your own and I want that understood. What I *can* offer is a better than fifty-fifty chance."

"Don't be a pack of fools, now!" roared Larsen above the hubbub of talk and eager exclamations. "There ain't a one of you that don't know how to get to south Texas by himself! Stevens here can't offer you a thing but low pay. Wait till we finish this job and there'll be plenty of time to make it down there with our pockets full!"

Pat understood his object clearly. The owlhoot leader was extremely reluctant to lose any of his men at a time when a slump in the force of numbers spelled the difference between success and defeat for his side in the railroad war. His shrewd argument might have carried weight but for one thing.

"What about that battalion of federal marshals we've had to fight off, Larsen?" an outlaw demanded truculently. "They've already given our boys a rough time—and they'll follow us plumb to Texas, and even into the cavalry!"

Hook spat a savage gust of invective, shouting the insurgents down. "Shut up!" he roared. "I'm the boss here—and I won't have no horse-driving shenanigans! I know you! The whole pack of you figure to grab that horse herd for yourselves, and run!" He was an imposing figure now, barrel chest thrust out and rough-maned head thrown back. "Alamo! Josh Pierce! Hod Lewis! . . . Grab these troublemakers and toss them—"

Turning roughly to wave an arm toward Pat and Sam Sloan, he abruptly broke off, noting with jarring surprise that Pat's Colt was out of the holster and trained squarely on his midriff.

4

"ANY OF YOU men want to leave with us?" Stevens rapped coolly, with Sloan stolidly backing him up. "You heard my proposition. I'll undertake to see you get away."

"By grab, I'm for a hombre that talks turkey!" cried Skurlock. He moved out to join the intrepid pair, far from being as careless of his actions as he appeared. "Not that I'm much worried about going where I want. How's for a little company, boys?"

A shock-headed man of forty-odd promptly stepped out. "Reckon I'm with you," he said.

"Okay, Jack. It's Jack Utter, Stevens," Skurlock threw over his shoulder. "He'll do to ride with. . . . You too, Alamo?" he asked as a third man moved forward. To Pat's surprise, the latter was the outlaw who had guarded him and Sam on the way here. "Step up, boys—this way to the army detail! Anyone else for hardtack and bullets?"

His rough-edged humor caused a chuckle or two among the outlaws. After a pause a fourth man lounged forward, casting a malignant look at his fellows to learn whether any would seek to contest his decision. He was Hod Lewis. Evidently they all knew him only too well, for only Larsen protested, his features choleric.

"Blast it, boys, lay off the jokes!' 'he ranted savagely. "You had your laugh—just don't carry this thing too far!"

"Never mind, Hook," Chunk Skurlock said smoothly. "Don't try to tell us what to do. I got paid yesterday, and I'll make you a present of what little I got coming. As of now," he stated with chilling finality, "you're not our boss any more."

Larsen erupted vehemently, trying to beat down this insurrection before any further losses to his fighting force were incurred. The owlhoots listened to the noisy arguments, grinning. Stevens narrowly measured the way the wind was blowing. Judging that Skurlock's bold effrontery would make this nervy play stick, there were now six against Larsen instead of two, with the other owlhoots apparently inclined toward neutrality. He was well enough satisfied with the outcome—four was the number of men he had hoped to pick up.

"All right. If we're all set let's pull out of here." Pat broke sharply through the angry talk. "Working hands are what I came for. I don't want anything else here."

"No you don't, Stevens!" The furious leader's bitter tirade was mostly for effect. "Hem 'em in, boys! We'll show this brassy horse trader he can't shanghai our men and get away with it!" He threw orders at several outlaws, striving to dominate the situation by sheer weight of authority.

To his chagrin his men merely looked at him stolidly, not actively refusing to comply, but simply neglecting to make any move whatever as Stevens and Sloan started to back away, accompanied by the hard-eyed quartet who had thrown in their lot with them.

"Just don't hold us up, boys—and we'll see you in the army," murmured Skurlock.

This time a few owlhoots guffawed in frank amusement. One made a facetious remark and the others, grimly entertained by this display of crust, laughingly allowed Pat, Sam, and their former comrades to detach themselves and move toward the horses. Larsen harangued his crew scathingly, with no appreciable result.

Not until he swung a leg over his bronc did Sam's secret anxiety subside in a surge of triumph. Yet even now he remained uneasy. "Get going, will you?" he growled at his companions in a fierce undertone. "They think it's funny now, but these birds could change their minds in a hurry. We won't hang around and wait for it!"

In a close group the six men swung their mounts away and started to leave. Hook Larsen, however, had two or three sycophants always ready to do his bidding. With the issue still undecided they had held off out of a healthy regard for their own skins. But glancing back, Pat now saw these men hurrying to mount their ponies. He read what it meant.

"Shake a leg, boys—unless you aim to stick around for breakfast. Larsen's breakfast," he added tersely. "Must be three or four in that bunch who fancy themselves as rifle shots. As Sam says, they may take it into their heads to only let us *think* we're making it away."

Chunk Skurlock scoffed the warning off. With typical hard assurance he laughed at the idea that they might be halted now. "That crowd knows what to ex-

pect from me," he boasted unblushingly. "More than
one is glad to see me go, I'll warrant you that!"

Sam scrutinized him admiringly. "I'll bet you're a
tough rooster at that," he said. "The Mexicans better
hunt their holes when they see you coming—"

Pat thought Sam was laying it on too thick and
gave him a warning glance. But Sloan had measured
his man with accustomed shrewdness. Chunk's barrel
chest expanded and he showed a wolfish grin.

"You're joshing me now, Sloan," he gave back. "But
you know it's the truth, too. You didn't make no mistake signing me up. . . . I am in, ain't I, Stevens?"
he broke off with ludicrous simplicity. "We're going
on this drive for real, and there *is* a chance at that
cavalry—?"

Pat's nod was curt. "You'll find it's real enough," he
promised. Privately he was beginning to wonder if
Chunk Skurlock would prove a handful to manage. But
almost certainly the burly, swaggering rough would
prove his worth at the first real brush with his own
kind.

"Some of them are taking out on our trail, Stevens,"
exclaimed Sam, gazing backward. Beyond the broken
rocks Pat could see that Larsen's confederates were
indeed coming this way fast, trying to outride and
flank them on either side.

Alamo had been keeping a close watch on this sur-
reptitious activity. "Ain't but three or four men behind
us, for all Larsen's loud talk," he said with a show
of uneasiness, "Something wrong about that—I don't
like it."

"Rather find the going tougher, would you?" queried
Sam.

"I get what he means," Jack Utter put in. "It's like
Larsen to let us think we're in the clear, and then
throw a stiff jolt into us later."

Stevens had left the beaten trail not far from the
owlhoot camp and was setting a course calculated to
take the maximum advantage of shelter offered by
brush and ledges. "You must know your way around

up here," he told Alamo. "Is there another way down off the mesa on this side, besides the one we came up?"

Alamo was about to reply when a carbine cracked distantly. The renegade ducked as the slug showered fragments of clipped brush down on his hat. "Yes, there is, Stevens," he bit off. "A trail that Hook won't be bothering to watch either."

Pat nodded. "Take us down that way," he directed. He kneed his pony forward in time to catch Sam's arm as the latter prepared to dismount, rifle in hand. "Never mind, Sam. Let them blow off a little steam," he advised. "Returning their fire now would only tip them off to the way we're going."

Sam grumbled under his breath but turned to follow Alamo's lead with the others. "What say—?" Skurlock prodded him.

"I hope we don't turn into a handful of those deputy marshals while we're ducking Larsen's crowd," Sam gave back tartly. "We got work to do, instead of high-jinking around in the brush!"

Skurlock grinned at his apparent tension. "Don't give it a thought. We'll have you country boys out of this in a jiffy."

True to prediction, under Alamo's guidance they soon found themselves following a twisting crevice which wound ever deeper into the rocks. In a little while the walls rose above their heads, and shortly thereafter Stevens was able to look out over the wide chasm of the lower range.

No further gunfire sounded nor did they again glimpse their pursuers. The trail dipped down sharply, leading over narrow ledges, where a slip meant a fall of hundreds of feet. In the lead, Alamo set a sedate pace and the horses slid and skated gingerly over the slick rock. Sam heaved a sigh when they struck the first rising shoulder under the mesa rim.

"What you don't have to go through to hire a few hands nowdays," he remarked. The owlhoots chuckled dryly.

"Where does that other trail come down off the top?" asked Pat.

Skurlock waved an arm. "Mile or two over south," he replied. "We'll swing wide, Stevens, and them wolf dogs of Larsen's will never scent us at all."

Once in the open Pat calmly took charge. Not accepting the outlaw's word for a thing, he made sure that they got away clean. It meant a longer ride, but he did not intend to have any complications later arising from persistent pursuit. It was well after midday, and miles to the south toward Powder Valley, before his vigilance relaxed.

"I expect we've seen the last of Larsen," he stated temperately. "We can shove on to the Bar ES now and get to work."

Jack Utter was not so sure about this, and Alamo seconded his doubts. "Don't forget that Larsen knows where we're heading for," he reminded Pat. "I've seen Hook crossed before, and it don't pay off—"

"Cut it out, you calamity howlers," interjected Skurlock. "Larsen's got no kick. We served notice, and we're on our own. Larsen naturally don't like it because he'll lose a commission on us; but the K.P. can't win. A week from now all them boys will wish they'd taken Stevens up. . . . I'll settle for driving horses, and maybe get me in that cavalry," he wound up virtuously.

The four owlhoots were all easy-going characters after their own fashion. Their chatter ran on as they rode. They speculated about what they would find awaiting them on the Texas coast, the progress of the expected war with Mexico, and a dozen other things. Chunk Skurlock was the most spirited of them all. His quips and gusty pronouncements kept the others in good humor. Pat and Sam quietly saw to it that they made good time.

With an early start that morning, they reached the northern boundary of Powder Valley in late afternoon and struck straight for Pat's Lazy Mare spread. They were in time to share a much-needed meal with the crew; and if the regular hands entertained a shrewd suspicion of the character of these hard-visaged strangers, they made no overt comment.

Resting only long enough after supper to enjoy a smoke, the little band shoved on south in the gathering twilight. Pat thought it prudent to swing wide around Dutch Springs, and it was crowding ten o'clock when they rode up to the little Bar ES. ranch. It suited Stevens that in the darkness no one had been able to trail them here or see them arrive.

There was a light in the log cabin, and the slab door crashed open as they clattered into the yard. Ezra strode out, his lanky figure casting an elongated shadow. He was followed closely by young Polk.

"That you, Stevens?" The one-eyed old rawhide voiced his gratification. "Didn't expect you before another day or so—knowing how slow Sam is." Ignoring his partner's instant vituperation, he peered at the shadowy forms of the men accompanying Pat and Sloan. "I see you picked up some hands as you said you would."

There was a brief bustle of movement as all dismounted and Polk Burnett helped turn the off-saddled ponies into a corral. Then Stevens led the four strangers into the light from the open door.

"Meet our new hands, Ez." He introduced the four by name. Greeting him with a grunted word or cursory nod, they made little of their own hardness since, with his lantern jaw, black patch and single piercing eye, Ezra looked every bit as tough and disreputable as themselves.

For his part Ezra looked them over deliberately. "Had experience with stock, I expect?" he wanted to know. It was plain that nothing else interested him.

"We've handled horses, if that's what you mean," Hod Lewis allowed mildly. Sloan scarcely bothered to supress a chuckle over this glaring understatement.

Ignoring the humor of the situation, Ez asked further questions until he was satisfied. Pat informed him they had eaten at the Lazy Mare on the way south.

"We can all stand coffee anyhow," the lanky man rejoined. He led the way in, and the fragrant odor soon filled the cabin. There was markedly casual talk while they drank. Pat noted the roundness of Polk Burnett's eyes as he sized up the newcomers. The puncher had no word for any of them. His sole observable reaction appeared to be one of perplexed disgust.

Sam at least had already established easy relations with the new hands by according them respectful attention and laughing at their jokes. Ez, on the other hand, appeared bent on demonstrating his cool authority from the start.

"Might as well turn in," he said when the tin cups were empty. "We may not have the chance later."

The four newcomers at once signified their preference for bedding down in the open. "We're used to it," Skurlock remarked briefly. "I know I won't rest easy in no cabin."

They filed out, taking their blanket rolls off the saddles propped against the wall, and in a matter of minutes unbroken quiet descended over the little horse ranch. Inside the cabin something seemed to be bothering Burnett. He stalled until Pat was almost ready to crawl in, and then spoke out.

"I was hoping all that about hiring outlaws was only talk," he said uneasily. "Wherever you scraped them up, it's plain those four are the real thing. Was it— necessary, Stevens?"

Pat shrugged, not bothering to answer directly. "Don't tell me you're worried about those nice boys?" he countered.

"You should worry plenty," blurted Polk. "You don't want anything to happen to that roan herd, I suppose. Or am I wrong about that?"

Listening, Ez snorted. "You ain't as smart as I thought," he thrust in. "Owlhoot or no owlhoot, boy, if they're taking pay from us they'll fight off the devil himself to guard them roans. You can count on that— because I aim to."

At the age when he knew everything, young Polk

struggled to be reasonable. "I sure hope you're right. It won't stop me from keeping an eye on that bunch every minute."

"You do that." Sam laughed. "It'll save us a lot of trouble."

Incensed by these jibes, Burnett allowed the subject to drop. True to his word, however, he was on the alert early the following morning and he did not miss the moment when Sam led the new hands around the cabin and waved toward the south pasture.

"There they are boys."

For a space there was dead silence. "Holy smoke," Chunk Skurlock swore then, fervently eyeing the magnificent roan herd. "If we'd only had the brains to steal this stuff, what a haul! Now we got to guard it."

Sam's laugh was untroubled. "That's what comes of making your deal sight unseen," he ribbed them. "You can be sure the army looked them broncs over—and they expect to see them again." It was plain that he delighted in dealing with these hardshells, and that they got a kick out of him as well.

Taking this in, Polk chafed indignantly. He whirled as Stevens came forward, and hot words burst from him. "Remember what I told you, Stevens! You'll have bad luck!"

The words were loud enough to attract the attention of the outlaws. They turned to look that way. "What's biting the kid?" asked Alamo casually. At a word from Pat the puncher's voice abruptly lowered. No more was said by the listeners, but it was plain that they were fully aware of Burnett's unconcealed suspicion.

"Let's stir our stumps here," Ezra broke in, striding briskly forward. "We got a long haul ahead of us, and there isn't any army check waiting for us here. As soon as we can throw our outfit together we'll be on the move."

5

EZRA'S DESIRE to be on the move at the earliest possible moment was all right with the others. Sam had long since got the range wagon greased and ready to roll, and while supplies were not overly plentiful they expected to pick up more on the trail rather than delay for the trip into Dutch Springs and back.

"We won't eat real good till we pick up a trail cook in the first town anyway." Sloan glanced keenly at the new hands. "Any of you birds know how to throw grub together?"

They looked surprised at the query. It seemed bad enough to descend to hard, poorly paid range work without having to cook in the bargain. No one answered until Skurlock spoke up. "Alamo is some sort of a half-baked cookee," he informed Sam with faintly malicious humor.

"That right, Alamo?"

The outlaw grimaced disgustedly. "I reckon—if you don't make nothing of a little indigestion," he allowed.

"Okay. I'll spell you," Sam offered, grinning. "You make one meal, and I'll make the next—till we sign on a regular cook. Is that fair?"

Obviously Alamo didn't think so, but he made no pointed protest and only grumbled to himself. He and Sam set about loading the wagon, aided by Burnett; and the chunky Bar ES partner could not help noting the owlhoot's patent dislike for the young puncher. Nothing Polk did suited Alamo. He made him move supplies from one place to another, rearranging the wagon half a dozen times; pretending Burnett was constantly in his way, he pushed and shoved him around. Polk's mouth tightened in a thin line, and he began to sweat.

"That gunslinger won't lay off of me," he muttered finally to Sam in tense-voiced exasperation.

Sam shrugged. "Your own fault, mostly. He heard you talking about him and the others. . . . Slug him one," was his advice. "Step on his toes good and hard. That'll wake him up."

Burnett reddened with helpless indignation. He well knew how much chance he would have with the case-hardened owlhoot. He was about to break into protest when Alamo came around the corner of the cabin. His malign glance sought out the puncher immediately.

"What are you dogging it for, punk?" he rasped irritably. "We ain't half done yet. Shake a leg, will you? I never yet saw a dang smooth-lipped kid that was worth a hoot."

Polk glared reproachfully at Sam and walked away. Alamo looked at Sam and coolly winked, but made no comment. Sam chuckled softly to himself.

It was crowding midday by the time they were ready to travel. In the saddle and primed for action, Ezra waved all hands forward and laid down terse instructions on the manner in which he expected the roan herd to be handled.

"No excuses will go," he warned the new hands flatly. "We go roughly a thousand miles to cover, and I don't figure to lose a single head of this stuff. Get that planted in your skulls and we'll get along fine."

It was scarcely the custom for hard-boiled outlaws to allow themselves to be talked to in exactly this manner, but clearly these men respected Ezra, feeling he was well within his rights. In a way it was a subtle compliment he paid them. Henceforth, his strict manner implied, their past was a private matter and they were to be regarded as simply hard-working range hands. Ez's single sharp eye was on them all as he gave them time to register any complaints at the outset.

"Are we ready to shove off?"

Skurlock waved a beefy hand with his usual irrepressible good humor. "That's five minutes shot to hell already. What are we waiting for, Ez?"

Ezra made a sign to Sam, who stood with one foot on the wheel hub of the camp wagon. Waving back, Sloan heaved himself up and settled on the groaning spring seat, gathering up the reins and putting his skittish team into motion. Rolling wide of the pasture fence, the vehicle set off.

"Okay, Polk!" Ez hailed the puncher. Burnett jumped his bronc to the south gate, swinging it wide. With Pat helping him, Ez started to urge the frisky roans onto open range. The four owlhoots were busy lining them out.

Within ten minutes the herd was in fairly orderly movement, striking south. For some miles the land in this direction was largely waste range. Although watered and fed, the roans did not like it, and they strove repeatedly to break back toward familiar territory.

For the better part of an hour all hands were busy keeping the herd in line. A spirit of deviltry seemed to animate the horses; again and again they sought to turn. More than one had to be pursued for a quarter-mile before it gave up and turned docilely in the desired direction, joining the others with an innocent air, only to look for the next opportunity to escape.

Pat was as energetic as anyone. It struck him that Polk Burnett was the busiest of all, dashing here and there to turn the insurgents. But for some reason the hardened outlaws were far from satisfied. "Snap it up, kid!" Hod Lewis yelled at Polk harshly. "You're doing a lot of riding and not much work."

Burnett turned on him protestingly. "I'm doing all one man can," he burst out. "What do you expect?"

"Use your head more and your hocks less, blast it!" bawled Lewis. "If you can't out-guess a stupid bronc this ain't no job for you."

Polk looked around appealingly, toward Ezra first and then Pat. Both men were busy at the moment and

appeared either to be paying no attention or not to
have heard. The puncher plunged into the work afresh.
When Alamo sailed into him later with simulated
wrath, and no notice was taken of it by Pat and the
partners, it dawned on Burnett that he was to be left
to his own devices in dealing with these men.

Skurlock was the only owlhoot who was not paying
much heed to the young fellow. Stevens saw him glancing around over the back trail from time to time.
"Something stuck in your craw, Skurlock?" he asked
finally. "Did you leave your toothbrush back there at
the ranch, or what?"

Chunk frowned and shrugged. "I laughed this off,
Stevens. But it ain't like Hook Larsen not to try to
make trouble. He's plumb mad at us."

Pat made no attempt to argue the point. "Larsen's
got his own fish to fry," he said. "In his boots, I'd be
thinking about something else besides us."

"What you don't know is that that railroad deal
was about to blow up in short order," Skurlock gave
back. "If Hook finds himself out of work, he'll start
thinking about us so fast it'll jolt you, Stevens."

It was Pat's turn to shrug. He surveyed the empty
miles of range all about before replying. "Time enough
for anything like that when it comes," he said at
length. "*I* don't expect to be made a fool of—and I've
got an idea you birds are pretty well able to take care
of yourselves."

It was the right thing to say. Skurlock's eyes brightened and his broad shoulders squared. "Glad you see
it that way," he allowed gruffly. "We'll just hope we
don't bring you no grief."

"Let Ez and me worry about that." Pat grinned. "I
knew what I was doing when I came after you fellows
and signed you on. I haven't yet decided that it was a
mistake."

"You're different from young Burnett then," said
Chunk.

The work kept them busy throughout the afternoon.
Toward evening, with the last rays of the setting sun

slanting level across the range, they reached a shallow creek with scanty graze scattered in the bottoms. Ez signified that they would pull up here for the night.

"Another day or two and the herd will be broken in," he averred. "Good thing, too. If I had to work that hard all the way to Texas I'd sell those plugs for chicken feed."

It was the better part of an hour before Sam caught up with the camp wagon. Alamo at once took charge of the pots and kettles, obviously disliking the task yet competent enough. Pat soon heard him ordering Burnett to drag in firewood, and Alamo gave the puncher a hard time until the pile was big enough to last for two nights at least.

All were so weary that they wolfed down the hearty supper in silence. Stevens instructed Polk to cover the first trick as night guard, a chore which would carry him away from the heckling owlhoots for a few hours. Sam relieved the puncher at midnight and came back to camp in time to throw together an early breakfast. "We'll have to load up with grub at Raton, Stevens," he announced as the men crawled out in the early half-light and hurriedly ate.

Pat nodded. "We'll pull up earlier that day, and you can pick up a cook in town while you're stocking up."

Although the roans proved ornery as ever until the sun came up to warm their backs, on this day they gave less trouble. Crew and herd alike showed signs of shaking down into an easy routine. The miles reeled off behind them steadily. Once again, fortunately, they struck a natural bedding ground in late afternoon.

Before dawn of the following day Ezra's yell brought all hands out of their blankets in a twinkling. "Come on, you sleepyheads!" he bawled. "Grab your chow and get it over with! Sloan's heading for town today and I don't want any stick-in-the-mud holding him up."

Breakfast was over in record time. Sloan hitched up

the wagon and took off before the herd was on the move, and the rest of them were on their way by the time the early sun flushed the top of the Spanish Peaks with rosy light.

They were at the southern end of the Culebra Range now. The trail rose steadily toward Raton Pass. Midday saw them at the edge of the Colorado Plateau; the craggy descent of the pass fell away to the south, the tawny New Mexican sage range opening to their view.

Dust whipped at them on the steady wind as the horses threaded the faint trails down the ragged benches and canyon tangents of the pass. Descending, they left the fresh coolness of spring behind, the hot breath of summer rising from the baked and barren flats below.

Reining up near Pat, Burnett pointed out a patch of buildings in the distance lying loosely scattered on the barren range, somewhat out of their course. "That's Raton, yonder, I expect—"

Pat nodded. "Sam followed the stage road, and he's either there now or near town. We're heading the broncs east to cut across the Panhandle and stick to good graze. He'll catch up with us some time tonight."

Dropping down from the pass, they set out across the range. Clumps of green willow marked the center of a long-sloped basin miles to the fore. It took an hour of steady travel to reach the spot. As Ezra hoped, there was a waterhole under the willows, so he told the others they would pull up here and wait for Sam. Long afternoon shadows had already enveloped the gray range.

The roans were watered and turned out to crop the scanty buffalo grass. As evening light paled, the men took up a notch or two in their belts and lit smokes to stave off hunger. It was almost dark when Jack Utter raised a cry. "Wagon coming!" he sang out.

It was Sam. It took him another twenty minutes to reach camp, and the men gathered eagerly as he drew up with a rattle and jingle of harness. The pudgy Bar

ES partner had a bearded old-timer on the seat with him, lanky and bent-shouldered.

"Meet Kip James, boys," Sam introduced the newcomer briskly. "He's our new cook. Wait till you throw your lip over one of his biscuits and you'll know why I hired him."

James got down from the wagon without a word, glanced toward the fire, and made his pronouncement. "Clear out of here, you saddle tramps, till I call you," he ordered brusquely.

Hastily moving away, and masking their grins, the owlhoots exchanged knowing glances. Skurlock nodded. "Knows his business, I reckon." Aware that the way to keep hard-working men satisfied was to feed them well, Sam had bought bountifully in Raton—the supper that night was plain but excellent.

The owlhoots had fitted smoothly into this job, all of them top hands. The only one Pat had reservations about from the beginning was Chunk Skurlock; and even Chunk had thus far given no cause for complaint. Tonight he was in top form, cracking jokes and keeping the others in an uproar of laughter. All showed signs of relaxing their wariness. Ezra was well pleased with the way things were going. Pat saw the new cook shrewdly appraising Skurlock and his companions; but old Kip proved to be habitually silent, and it was impossible to read his thoughts.

They got a good start next day, and with Sam and Alamo released from the wagon, the work went smoothly. Another day saw them over the line into Texas, the salty roans offering little difficulty.

On the third day below Raton a long line of dun-colored bluffs appeared, extending raggedly across the horizon. All but young Polk recognized this as the northern edge of the Llano Estacado. The bluffs remained remote and hazy for many hours, gradually looming higher. Toward midday the southern sky darkened slowly and ominously; a baleful halo rimmed the ragged bluffs ahead. Ezra looked that way repeatedly, shaking his head.

"Dust storm blowing up," he tersely answered Burnett's look of uneasy inquiry. "Watch the broncs close, boy. They could stampede to hell and gone in this."

The sky turned deep brown. The breeze stiffened, hot and scorching; the brush nodded and jerked in the rising gusts. Polk's concern grew. He saw Skurlock yelling and waving to his friends, without making out a word that was said; but they started pushing the roans forward at an increased pace. Soon they were thundering toward the bluffs on a dead run. Polk heard an eerie wail on the wind now, and dust riding the gale made him blink and choke. The others were hurriedly tying kerchiefs over their faces.

Suddenly a jagged streak of lightning tore across the alarming pall of blackness. Strangely muffled thunder crashed and rolled across the heavens. In a flash the horses broke, striving to turn back. Ezra's bellowing cry was unintelligible, but every man raced to cut off the rebels. Somehow they succeeded. Ten minutes later, racing on in terror, the herd thundered close under the lofty bluff. Here the tearing wind dropped to swirling gusts; but thickening sand and dust made sight all but impossible in the murky gloom.

Slowly but surely Stevens and Sloan turned the running broncs, and at last they came to a halt, milling uneasily. "Hold 'em right here!" Ezra sang out. "It's our only chance!"

More lightning blazed. But now the roans were strangely subdued; heads lowered, they seemed to depend on their mounted guardians. To Burnett's astonishment, despite the lightning and the billowing, low-hung clouds, only a scattering of raindrops fell, quickly ceasing. An hour dragged by, the dark pall gradually passing on overhead. Although the full force of the wind was cut off under the bluff, it continued to wail weirdly in the upper sky. The penetrating dust swirled and eddied, causing the men to gag and sneeze. The horses were in no better case, wheezing and tossing, thrusting their noses between their fore-legs.

The sky lightened toward evening, but it was late before Kip James had coffee ready, and he did not bother preparing food. A few biscuits were passed around, and even these tasted like sand. The gritty dust got into everything.

There was little attempt at rest during the night. The next day dawned bleak and blustery, the heat stifling. No attempt was made to move on; but with daylight old Kip whipped together a meager meal which the hands choked down, and during the day those who were able snatched brief intervals of rest.

The ensuing night proved less of an ordeal, with the wind dying out at long last and the omnipresent, pene-trating dust slowly settling. Dawn of the following day found all eager to thrust on. After the first decent meal in over thirty hours they set the broncs into motion, trailing them up one of the winding washes gashing the bluff, and two hours later were making fair time over the broad flat expanse of the plain.

It was Ezra whose sharp eye noted the weary out-laws getting their heads together during the morning. Plainly they were soberly discussing something. They looked ahead from time to time with obvious uneasi-ness. Finally Hod Lewis reined back to accost Pat.

"We catch on now why you hired us, Stevens," he said flatly.

6

Pat GLANCED at the owlhoot without surprise. "Why is that, Hod?" He seemed only mildly curious.

Lewis waved a hand about the level plain, marked only by brush and faraway clumps of cottonwood. "This is horse-thief country all through here," he said plainly. "Dang it, Stevens, Tascosa's less than a day's drive away—the toughest town in Texas!"

While this was a manifest exaggeration, it was true that Tascosa had long been notorious in a territory peculiarly given over to lawlessness. Pat brushed the warning aside, however.

"Those days are over now," he said. "We'll get through."

Hod turned away, shaking his head, and it was evident that Pat's assurances did not relieve the uneasiness of the owlhoots.

Sam Sloan realized this when his jests left them singularly indifferent. "What's eating these birds?" he found occasion to ask Stevens.

Pat briefly repeated the exchange with Hod Lewis. Sam snorted. "Why, this is what we hired them hardshells for," he scoffed. "Don't tell me they're heated up over a handful of their own kind!" Yet the possibility left the stocky man thoughtful. Thereafter he made it his business to query one or another of the outlaws. It was Chunk Skurlock who finally told him what he wanted to know.

"Stevens thinks there's nothing to fuss about," Chunk said dourly. "But for your information, Sloan, Tascosa ain't the ghost town he thinks it is."

Ezra came jogging forward as they talked. He lis-

50

tened alertly to the end, and put in his own gruff query. "What makes you so sure of that, Skurlock?"

"I happen to know." Chunk gave him a shrewd look. "Right now there's a bunch of the boys holed up at Tascosa trying to figure out how to get into the U. S. cavalry, same as we are. A big bunch," he added significantly.

Ezra scratched his grizzled hair under the black flat-brim. This news was more than enough to give pause for sober thought. Except for widely scattered ranches, a few of them famous brands, the Texas Panhandle was sparsely settled. Whether they liked it or not, it would be necessary to go through Tascosa to pick up supplies before striking out into the barren wasteland to the south. Even with their owlhoot guard, if Skurlock was truthful, it would be considerable risk.

Ez would not give Chunk the satisfaction of hearing him reveal his secret concern. "We'll have to figure out something," he said, with a shrug. "Better get back here in the drag and help Utter shove them along, Skurlock—"

Chunk did as he was told without comment but the partners did not let the matter drop. Discussing it soberly as they road, they concluded that Tascosa might well constitute a threat which they could not afford to ignore.

"We better bat this around with Pat," proposed Sam.

No opportunity presented itself during the afternoon. But in camp that evening Ezra called Stevens aside. The owlhoots were used to seeing the trio confer from time to time and paid no particular heed. At the moment their attention was fixed on hazing young Burnett. Striving to ignore them, Polk was exhibiting his own brand of stoicism.

Pat looked from Sam to Ezra, his glance quizzical. He thought he understood the reason why they had called him aside. "If you want me to put a stop to that business the answer is No," he said briefly. "Sooner or later Burnett has to learn to get along with those hombres. No time like the present."

"No, it's about something else," Sam hastened to inform him. "It's those boys themselves, Stevens. We don't like the way they're talking. It wouldn't be at all impossible for them to up and pull out on us without notice." He cited the frank unrest of the outlaws at the approach to Tascosa.

"Oh hell—" began Pat shortly. But Ezra caught him up.

"Wait till you hear this, boy." He repeated Skurlock's news of a considerable gathering of outlaws at the isolated trail town, ending with Chunk's tacit prediction of trouble. "I don't think they aim to walk out on us," he said. "They're as bothered about these roans as we are. So it must mean something."

"Don't you get it? We're asking them to buck their own friends," Sam threw in urgently.

"I get it all right," drawled Pat. "Just why did you suppose I suggested hiring them in the first place?"

They talked it over without getting anywhere. Even if Tascosa were by-passed by the herd, the conclusion was, the arrival in town of a supply wagon would tip the idle owlhoots off to what was afoot. It presented a knotty problem.

"No, we won't circle around anything," Pat ruled firmly. "We'll ram straight through or not at all." He fell into a thoughtful mood and looked up. "I think I've got it," he announced.

"You have?" Sam looked blank and sounded skeptical. "What's your idea?"

Pat held them with a confident gaze. "It's simple. You didn't take time to road-brand these army roans, and it's a good thing you didn't. There must be a small ranch or two a few miles out of Tascosa," he explained. "We'll make arrangements with one of them to use their corrals, and we can slap the US army brand on every last bronc." He waited triumphantly for their approving response. "Don't you see it? No owlhoot will dare vent that brand. They know the government would hound them clear to Montana and never let up!"

"Hey, you got a point there." Sam took fire immediately. "This ought to set that Tascosa crowd back on their heels—and our boys will get a kick out of parading the brand under their noses."

"Could be." Ez grunted, by no means as completely reassured as his squat partner. "It's worth a try anyhow—"

"Tascosa can't be more than thirty miles or so. I'll shove on ahead tomorrow," Sam said. "If there's a little spread outside of town somewhere I'll find it."

"And never mind explaining the whys and wherefores either, Sam," Pat cautioned. "Just ask if we can rent their corrals for two or three days. You shoudn't have any trouble."

Weary of giving Polk a hard time, the rough-barked hands were turning in for the night. Jack Utter, serving as night guard, had already saddled a fresh bronc from his string and ridden out to watch the herd. Once Kip James got the supper utensils washed up the fire was allowed to die down, and dreaming silence settled over the camp.

The moon tonight seemed enormous; the stars glittered in swarms; the mute unbroken peace presented a sharp contrast to the troubles of men. On the move early the following morning, the outlaws wore a preoccupied expression as a hasty breakfast was finished and the herd got in motion. Pat knew they fully expected to reach Tascosa that day, and if they made no overt protest, their faces were grim and taciturn.

All were surprised late in the morning when Stevens gave the order to halt the roans. They thought they understood when Sloan, after talking briefly with Ezra and Pat, turned his horse's head and road away alone. Oddly enough, it was young Polk who questioned this move.

"Somebody ought to side Sam if he's barging into Tascosa alone," he told Stevens. "How do we know what he'll run into there?"

Pat's smile was easy. "Sam's been around for quite a while," was his only response. "He'll get along."

Skurlock overheard the exchange. "It's none of my

affair, Stevens. But the kid's right," he said. "Ain't a one of us that wouldn't be ready to go along with Sloan. We could maybe help," he added meaningfully.

"I'm sure of it, Chunk," Pat agreed calmly. "We'll count on you when your turn comes."

Baffled, the burly owlhoot turned away. But it was plain from the occasional comments they exchanged and the close watch they kept on the sundrenched plain while they waited that he and his companions were concerned.

The afternoon dragged away and it was sunset when Sam came jogging back, fully as self-confident as ever. Eating supper at the moment, the crew set their tin plates aside. "How'd you make out, Sam?" demanded Alamo.

Sloan flopped a pudgy hand. "Fine and dandy," he vouchsafed. "We'll haul up on the little Saw Log outfit on Cheyenne Creek."

He did not elaborate, falling into low-voiced conversation with his lanky partner, and the hands looked at one another uncertainly. "They probably aim to lay out at this ranch while they look the situation over in Tascosa," hazarded Hod Lewis. Hod Lewis was on night guard that night, and the other owlhoots were busy putting their own heads together in anxious speculation. Whatever the conclusion was, they remained markedly sober and crawled into their blankets early.

Next morning started off much like a routine day, with the roans on the trail before full daylight. Although they did their work as diligently as ever, Skurlock and his friends kept an alert watch to the fore.

By midmorning a long wavering line of willow and cottonwoods put in an appearance. Soon afterward Sloan briskly indicated a change of course. A couple of miles brought them to a straggling, shallow creek which Sam said was the Cheyenne. Turning to follow its course, they came presently within sight of several large corrals built of skinned poles. No life was to be seen anywhere about, nor was there any pasture fence; but the corrals showed signs of recent use.

At an inquiring look from Ezra, Sam nodded. "This is Saw Log," he announced. "We can use these pens as long as we need to."

Ez looked the setup over. "Pretty fair at that," he observed approvingly. "We can graze the broncs on the creek bottom, and turn a bunch in the big corral as we work them."

Skurlock came riding forward as they talked, Alamo at his side. "What's this?" the big outlaw rumbled, waving his hand about. "It ain't Matagorda by a long shot—"

Pat turned to face the pair. "We'll be here for two or three days," he informed them. "We're acting on your advice, Skurlock. You remember you said something back at the Bar ES about road-branding this stuff. We'll do that now."

"Why now, Stevens—and just here?" Chunk failed to understand, his tone rough with displeasure. "How far is Tascosa from here, anyhow?"

It was Sam who answered. "She lays up the Canadian five or six miles, Chunk." He indicated the direction.

Still Skurlock failed to comprehend. "You call this a ranch?" He cast a glance about the lonely spot. "Ain't a thing around here but these abandoned corrals!"

"Oh, the Saw Log is a quarter-mile down the creek there. Those folks won't bother us; and while we're doing our work we needn't bother them."

"Hang it, Stevens! This is just what I warned you about," exclaimed Skurlock. "It'll take time to brand them salty roans! Only a whoop and a holler from Tascosa like this, those boys in town could show up here in a hurry. It simply don't make sense!"

"Look, Skurlock." Pat straightened him out in a hurry. "If you think we're trying to get you into a row with your friends, forget it. This is a job we've got to do. We'll do it the way we have to." He paused to re-guard the pair levelly. "You hired on of your own free will. You do the work; we'll do the thinking," he instructed them bluntly.

Skurlock looked disgusted but calmed down. "If we're left to do our work, okay. I sure hope you got your next move all figured out," he grumbled as he turned away.

The crew was busy running thirty or forty head of horses into the big main corral. Pat asked Ezra if anybody had tossed two or three running irons into the camp wagon at starting and learned that this detail had been overlooked. "Ride into Saw Log, will you, and pick up a couple of irons," he instructed Hod Lewis briefly. "Tell them I'll personally make sure they get back home."

Sam started to say something as Lewis raised a hand in acquiescence and turned away. "What was it, Sam?" Pat asked.

Sloan waved it away. "Never mind—"

Stevens was to remember the incident later, but at the moment his attention was attracted to where Alamo was building a branding fire in the corral, ready to start work as soon as Lewis returned with the running irons.

"What kind of a road brand are you sticking on these roans, Stevens?" Jack Utter queried. It did not escape Pat that the others paused, waiting to catch the answer.

"We'll run the US brand on now," he returned coolly. "It'll save us and the cavalry both trouble—"

"*What*—" bawled Utter in an outraged tone. "You're running the government brand on these critters—here? Stevens, are you crazy?" he demanded incredulously.

Pat saw the flush of anger crawl across Alamo's set jaws as well. He had expected some grumbling over the use of the army brand, but nothing like this.

"That's right—we'll burn the US iron on every head," he retorted evenly. "Why not? This is already army stock by signed agreement. You understood that. Any harm in advertising the fact?"

"*I* think so," retorted Utter flatly. "I think you're asking for trouble, mister. I don't like it—and the rest of the boys won't either!"

Stevens pretended keen interest, watching him narrowly. "Let's get this straight," he said deliberately. "You certainly knew these roans were for the army. And you and the others agreed to help us deliver them. Is that right, or am I mistaken?"

Jack nodded grudgingly. "I'm not arguing that—"

"Then what is your point, Jack? Are you hoping to keep it a secret?"

Utter's corded visage darkened with exasperation. "We agreed to deliver the stock, Stevens, so let's get about it!" he roared. "We didn't bargain for no all-summer job, or any fancy work either. . . . I thought you was in a hurry to get this stuff to Matagorda!"

The longer they talked the more Pat was convinced the men were concealing something which weighed heavily on their minds. He was on the point of trying to drag it out into the open when a thudding of hoofs on the prairie sod came to their ears. They turned to find Hod Lewis racing forward. He had several running irons across his saddle-bow, and it was plain he had accomplished his errand; but as he swept close all saw that his stern face was portentous.

"What kind of a deal is this?" he burst out harshly, hauling his mount back on its haunches and raking them all with blazing eyes. "There ain't nothing but two women at that ranch house! Is that supposed to be our protection around here, or what?"

Sam Sloan had observed Hod's approach and ridden forward to hear what was said. "Yes, that's Trinket Martin's ranch," he interjected. "She's been running Saw Log since old Buff Martin got thrown from a horse here last season. I got her story when I was here to make my deal. The other woman is Thankful Feather, Trinket's old mammy." He broke off, staring at Lewis inquiringly. "What's your squawk?"

"We don't want no part of it, that's what," bawled

Hod. "If we got to fool around branding broncs there won't be no time for nursing womenfolks, I'll tell you that right flat!"

If this was an ultimatum, Sam failed to recognize it as such. "Nonsense," he said. "Don't make a mountain out of a molehill. Do your work and we won't ask anything else from you. The Martin girl can use a few dollars for the use of her corral," he went on hardily. "Don't tell me you big bad wolves begrudge her that?"

It was the one avenue of attack that could take the wind out of the owlhoots' protest. "Well—" began Lewis, but he was already routed. Scowling, he and Alamo turned away.

7

FULLY CONSCIOUS THAT every extra hand would help to shorten the time required to brand the roans, Stevens diplomatically accosted old Kip James on the subject.

"We'll be here two or three days anyway, maybe longer," he said. "Why not drive on to Saw Log, Kip? That way the wagon will be out of the dust. Sam says there's a bunch of cottonwoods down there. It'll mean shade and plenty of wood too."

The grizzled cook regarded him out of keen hooded eyes. "Two or three days? Why so long, Stevens?" Like all crusty camp cooks he was deeply suspicious of any offer to contribute to his personal comfort.

Pat shrugged. "These roans are plenty hard to handle," he pointed out. "Most of them have never been broken. It'll take three men to hog-tie one of those babies; and with a hot burn on their hip they'll come up fighting. We'll be able to use all the hands we can scrape up." He paused briefly, then thrust on as if he had a new idea. "How would you like sitting a saddle for a day or two?"

"I hired out to cook." James frowned scornfully. "Look fine bulldogging one of them steel-spring man-traps, wouldn't I?" he growled.

"No, I mean it." Pat spoke with sober earnestness. "We'll need at least two guards with the herd while the rest are busy branding. I may be able to arrange for those women to cook our meals; and if you'll ride guard, that will release another man from the corral. Of course we won't eat as good for a while," he went on smoothly. "But we can stand that if it puts us on the trail again a day sooner."

He was using the right arguments. Like many another trail cook, old Kip secretly regretted the advancing years which had virtually put him on the shelf. To be deftly flattered on his cooking set well with him also. Ingrained stubbornness prevented him from agreeing too readily, even to his own advantage.

"Well, I don't know—I'm plumb out of practice now, Stevens. I'll probably get all stove up."

Pat saw that he was privately eager for the chance. His laugh was short. "That's a good one," he scoffed lightly. "You'll probably ride the rest of us into the ground." He broke off. "Shall I ride in and talk to that girl?"

Old Kip loved being asked for advice. His assent was gruff. "I'll do what I can to help out," he allowed.

Pat's thanks was anything but casual. As it happened, James was an indifferent cook at best; and while this did not greatly matter, Stevens welcomed the opportunity to enjoy even a few really good home-cooked meals. "I won't forget this, Kip," he promised. "I'll shove on down to the ranch right now, and if it's okay with those women you can start riding guard in the morning."

He was as good as his word. The men were getting

the branding started in the big corral under Ezra's direction when Pat set off down the creek.

As Sam had said, he found the little Saw Log spread a quarter of a mile below. The ranch house was a comfortable, sprawling, low-roofed log structure situated on a flat beside Cheyenne Creek, and pleasantly shaded by gnarled cottonwoods. A flutter of bright calico caught his eye as he rode into the yard, and he saw a thin, whip-hard elderly Negro woman hanging clothes on a line.

"Howdy, ma'am," At first glance Pat instinctively approved of Aunty Thankful. Neat as a pin, with thinly set lips and bright sharp eyes, she was the obvious owner of both pride and character. "I'm Pat Stevens—with the horses. I expect my friend Sam has already met you. Is Miss Martin home?" Respectfully removing his hat, he waited for the answer.

Thankful Feather scrutinized him keenly, and he got the feeling that she had taken his measure completely. "Good day to you, sir. . . . Yes, she's around." She turned toward the log ranch house, calling out shrilly, "You—Trink!"

A moment later a very good-looking, brown-eyed and brown-haired girl of possibly twenty appeared in the kitchen door. "Yes, Aunty—?" Her eye fell on Stevens and she stepped out into the yard with a friendly, frank nod. "How do you do—" she began.

"He's with that herd out yonder, Trink, and a deal politer than that last range trash that practically jerked our branding irons out of my hands," said Aunty Thankful.

Pat returned Trinket Martin's smile and dismounted. "That was Hod Lewis, ma'am—one of the hands," he said. He introduced himself briefly. "Since we'll be neighbors for a few days I decided to pay my respects."

Trink Martin proved easy enough to talk with. It did not take Pat long to size up her situation, glancing about the tiny Saw Log. Old Buff Martin had left her barely comfortable. Three or four fair horses stood switching flies in a near-by corral, and it was plain that she did her own work, submitting to the somewhat testy domination of the older woman with calm patience.

"Fine range along the creek here, from what I've seen," Pat commented easily. "I suppose you're running a few head of steers?"

"Not just now." Trinket looked uneasy for a moment. "Conditions are—somewhat unsettled," she said evasively. "I sold off our beef this spring and haven't found exactly the right buy."

"You mean you're waiting out those pesky owlhoots there in town, honey," put in Aunty Thankful tartly. "No point in asking them to steal us blind! Why don't you tell the man?" She looked fiercely indignant as she ended, grumbling under her breath.

Faint color touched Trinket's tanned cheeks as she met Pat's gaze. "I'm sure Mr. Stevens doesn't want to hear about our troubles, Aunty," she murmured.

"As it happens, it does interest me," Pat responded quickly. He explained his hope of having them prepare meals for the trail crew. "If I knew you were busy with your own chores I'd hesitate to ask such a thing. As it is, maybe you won't mind earning a few extra dollars."

Aunty Thankful's groan was loud. "The work will fall on me," she complained vigorously. "And them worthless hands ain't a bit better than all the ornery scoundrels in Tascosa. I'm sure of it!"

Trinket joined in Pat's laugh. "Nonsense, Aunty," she chided softly . "They're just hard-working trail drivers. With Mr. Stevens in charge there's not a thing to worry about. And you're perfectly aware I'll help you with the work."

The old woman shrugged her thin shoulders. "We need the money," she vouchsafed plainly. "The good Lord only knows how you'd get along without me, child." She favored Stevens with a remarkably venomous glance. "Will your scalawags be showing up here tonight?"

"If that's okay, Aunty. And thanks a heap," Pat said.

Her nod was cursory. "We'll run out of grub directly," she predicted gloomily.

"Oh, I'll take care of that," he hastened to assure her. "I'll have the cook wagon brought down. We'll have to pick up supplies in Tascosa before we shove on anyway."

Aunty Thankful brightened somewhat at this. But she was making no concessions. "Well, get about it then," she directed, returning to her own work with vigor. Pat thanked Trinket and a few minutes later was on his way back to the herd.

"Drive the wagon right down to Saw Log," he instructed old Kip at the corral. "In the morning you're just another saddle tramp while we get this work pushed along."

The alacrity with which the old rawhide complied attested to his readiness. Sam hailed Pat's arrangements with satisfaction. The branding was already going forward briskly, clouds of dust billowing up from the corral where the roans squealed and stamped about and the men vented harsh cries and curt orders.

"We'll work right on till dusk, boys," Sloan sang out, climbing the corral bars to get their attention. "We're eating at the ranch tonight, and old Kip will pitch in and help us. Him and Polk can hold the herd while the rest of us slap on the irons."

They took the news indifferently, the hard, dirty work going steadily on. It was late when they knocked off, with some two score horses branded. Pat remained at the herd with young Burnett while the rest splashed through a hasty wash-up at the creek and headed for supper at the ranch. It was the better part of an hour before Sam and Alamo rode out to relieve the pair.

"How did it go?" Stevens asked the stocky little man.

"Fine and dandy." Sam slapped his belly resoundingly. "Best eats in a blue moon, boy," he averred with satisfaction.

"No trouble at all, eh?"

Sam looked at him with comprehension. "No. . . . If you mean Skurlock and the boys, Stevens, they caught on right away that that old mammy had them pegged. They had a lot of fun joshing her. But she can hold her own, too."

Pat grinned. "I'll buy that. It may come to whether they can or not." He turned in the saddle, raising his voice. "Let's go, Burnett!"

It was Polk's first look at Saw Log as they rode in. He glanced about casually, dismounting in the yard, and started to wash up at the bench outside the kitchen door. Aunty Thankful peered out at the pair. "Get a move on. This supper is hot right now," she barked.

"Yes, ma'am. Coming directly," Burnett replied, winking at Pat. Stevens saw the young puncher abruptly straighten up the moment they were inside.

"You must be Mr.—Burnett." Trink Martin looked him up and down almost indifferently, motioning toward the laden table. "You can sit there."

Polk moved that way with alacrity, nearly knocking his chair over in getting his legs under the table. Watching in amusement, Pat saw his eyes get big. Polk looked at the girl earnestly as if forgetting where he was.

"All right—go ahead and eat," said Trinket with a briskness that seemed to belie her own brief uncertainty. Polk hastened to comply, acting more self-conscious with every passing moment.

Not missing a thing, Aunty Thankful glowered at him in frank disfavor, banging fresh dishes down between the two men brusquely. Pat found it difficult to promote conversation, since neither Trinket nor Burnett allowed themselves more than a brief word or two. It was clear the pair were keenly aware of each other. Polk ate less than usual and seemed relieved when he got outside once more. He shoved off for the horse herd ahead of Stevens, who delayed for a word or two with the women. Pat had watched precisely this sort of situation develop before, and he understood the puncher's anxiety to avoid being twitted about it.

The owlhoots kept to themselves that night before turning in; they appeared to be arguing something with unusual earnestness. "They ain't happy about our using the US brand on these broncs," Ezra observed to Pat.

Alamo and Hod Lewis saddled up and moved out to take the first trick as night guards, and the camp settled down. Nothing marred the star-shot serenity of the night. Tumbling out in the early dawn, Pat and Sloan took charge of the horses while the others rode in to breakfast.

Although Burnett was silent again at the table, the others did not have any trouble finding something to say. It was Skurlock who started the branding discussion afresh. "You're asking for trouble, Ezra," he told the lanky man flatly. "Just don't forget I told you."

Ez shrugged, scrutinizing them all shrewdly. "You're just hoping your Tascosa pals will steal some of those broncs," he jested.

Chunk answered dourly. "No. Didn't I say you should have pushed right on past Tascosa? What you don't get is that Hook Larsen could have sent word ahead to have us stopped here."

The fact that Ezra had never met Larsen personally did not help to intimidate him now. "That bunch at Tascosa is all trying to get in the cavalry," he scoffed. "They could turn up riding our roans for Uncle Sam."

"Not likely." Skurlock quickly disabused him, shaking his head. "Larsen didn't tell Stevens those boys tried to get in the army once and got turned down. Word has gone out that any known outlaw who tries to enlist will land in the guardhouse. To them that US brand is like a red rag to a bull. . . . Hell, Ez," he said harshly, "they might even try to grab this herd just to make sure the army don't get it!"

It was all bad news to Ezra, even though he refused to acknowledge as much. Back at the herd later, he told Stevens briefly what Chunk had said. Pat listened carefully but remained unmoved.

"Skurlock is being franker than I expected," he said. "I'm a little surprised about him. Whether he's right or wrong, I think those boys will stick no matter what comes." He paused. "We'll still do it our way."

Ez did not take time then to discuss it further. But during the morning while the branding was proceeding in the corral, he found occasion to accost Pat afresh.

"Looks like we're being watched, Stevens." He waved toward the surrounding range.

Pat had already taken note of a stray rider or two, passing by at a distance but obviously watching the activities in the Saw Log corral. Glancing about now, he spotted still another. His nod was curt. "Word was bound to get around."

Others were aware they were being spied on. Stevens saw Polk Burnett glancing repeatedly toward the ranch and guessed what was in his mind. But with work to be pushed, there was no time for vagrant fears.

Pat was taking a turn at the branding fire early in the afternoon when Hod Lewis and Utter ran a fresh bunch of roans in through the corral gate. It took expert riding to herd the horses off into a corner of the corral while they awaited their turn That done, Lewis allowed his mount to drift toward the fire while Utter held the broncs.

"Did you know old Kip is watching the horses out there on the flat all by himself?" the owlhoot demanded.

Pat straightened up. "Isn't Burnett out there with him?" he returned sharply.

"No, he ain't." Lewis evinced disgust. "If you ain't got it yet, he's at the ranch chasing that girl, Stevens!"

The accusation jarred Pat's good nature. "All right.

Go right on with your work, Lewis," he retorted. He did not spare the time to look into the matter, nor did he do much thinking about it. Hod Lewis, however, could not get it out of his mind. Having subbed as a wrangler for an hour, the outlaw was released to pick up another bronc from his string. He ran into Alamo, also saddling a fresh mount, and growled out his story.

Alamo's eyes narrowed. "Like that, eh? We can't let the kid run a blazer on us while we work, Hod."

Resolve was born in them both as they exchanged a meaningful glance. They swung astride and set off briskly for Saw Log, being careful to avoid observation as they rode away from the corrals.

"Is that Burnett's bronc there in the yard?" muttered Alamo, as they neared the cottonwood-shaded ranch.

But there were three saddle horses waiting beside the log ranch house when they rode close. Neither spoke; they examined the strange horses carefully and left their own concealed from sight as they dismounted.

The kitchen door stood ajar and harsh voices sounded from within. Alamo slipped quickly along the log wall and paused just short of the door, with Lewis close at his heels. The voices grew louder. They heard Trinket Martin's distressed protest. They reached the door at a stride and paused there unseen—to find Polk Burnett in the middle of the kitchen floor, holding two hard-faced men at bay under the poised muzzle of his six gun.

8

ALAMO INSTANTLY RECOGNIZED the hardened, conscienceless pair smiling sardonically at young Burnett, their beady eyes locked on his every move—and so did Lewis. They were Bat Hanlon and Harve Lovat, old acquaintances of the outlaw trail, and more recently notorious as hired assassins of the railroad wars.

"Give us one reason why we don't belong here as much as you do," Hanlon hurled at Polk with cool venom.

"Because I say you are not wanted!" cried Trinket stoutly, standing flushed and defiant beside her Aunty Thankful.

Burnett's Colt twitched suggestively. "You heard the lady. Get out before I blast you out!"

Lovat rasped his stubbly jaw, his chuckle mirthless and virulent. "We'll probably go—after the lady sends you and the rest of your sneaky crew packing. . . . Didn't we warn you not to let these hombres stay, ma'am?" he flung at Trinket with a show of reasonableness. "There's a lesson has to be taught here. Too bad this handsome young fellow had to get in the way!"

"Let go of my arm, Trink," snapped Aunty Thankful. "Lemme get my broom. I'll sweep this trash out—"

Her aging face, set in ugly lines now, might have been carved from unyielding ebony. Alamo saw that Trinket had the old woman in a firm grip, restraining her from decisive, and surely disastrous, violence.

"Be quiet, Aunty." The girl possessed amazing self-control. Her white face showed that she read the potential evil of this pair.

But Hanlon only laughed. "Let the old bat go," he rasped. "She looks about ready to be riding a broomstick! I'll help her get started—"

His words were cut off sharply at the warning click of Burnett's six gun. "Will you pull out of here?" Polk blazed at them.

"Oh well. If you're plumb anxious about it." But instead of turning away, the renegades began to move apart. Alamo read the calculated treachery in their smooth co-operation. The pair were perfectly capable of shooting the puncher down before he was fully aware of what was happening.

Determined to break this up in a hurry, Alamo waited no longer. He stepped quietly through the door, halting in plain view of the wily pair, thumbs hooked in his cartridge belt. "What's the trouble, Bat?" he asked the red-haired Hanlon carelessly. "Can't you find the way to the door?"

Bat and Harve Lovat froze briefly, their faces going wooden. "If it ain't old Alamo," said Lovat. "And Hod, too. How's that for a couple of old buddies turning up unexpected!"

Hod Lewis, the biggest man in the room, shook his head stolidly. "Not a thing accidental about it, Harve. No more than your being here. Did I hear somebody say you were leaving?"

Hanlon's crooked grin flashed out. "I reckon you did, now you remind me," he grunted. Hard as he was, he had no intention of tangling with these new arrivals. "We'll see you around, Hod. We didn't know who it was here; but seeing it's you and Alamo, chances are we'll find the time to drop around again. We'll tell Lasher you're here anyway," he added carelessly.

Neither of the owlhoots revealed an awareness of the ominous threat that lay under the impudent cover-up. "You do that—some time when we're not busy," Alamo returned evenly. "Your broncs are waiting just outside—"

"So they are."

Silence fell as the intruders made for the door with elaborate casualness and shuffled out. Hod Lewis followed methodically, watching them mount and ride away. Relief left the two women inarticulate for a moment. Aunty Thankful was the first to recover her aplomb. "Never thought I'd be saying this," she allowed severely. "But I'm obliged to you and your friend, Mister Alamo."

Alamo laughed soundlessly at her tone. "Give the devil his due, eh?" His attention returned almost at once to Polk, still watching from the door. "I sure don't savvy you, boy," he brought out bluntly. "After the ribbing you taken lately without a peep, you faced up to them man-eaters in fine style." There was undisguised admiration in his gruff tone.

"He was brave," said Trink breathlessly. "None of us had any idea you and Mr. Lewis were anywhere about."

"Brave and foolish—don't overlook that," added Hod, stepping into the kitchen in time to catch her remark. "Don't know but what I like you better for it, Burnett," he added.

Polk waved his words away impatiently. But it was plain that this frank admiration gratified him. "It had to be done," he said tersely. "Stevens should've seen this coming."

"You were smart," Alamo agreed. "Almost smart enough to be ready for what that pair would have handed you in another minute or two."

"I *was* right though," Polk said stoutly. "There wasn't time to argue Pat or Ezra into posting a guard here at the ranch."

"We'll point that out to Stevens," Lewis affirmed. "In fact you can stay right here while I go after him."

Trinket looked as though she would have protested. But a glance at Burnett's hard young face silenced her. It was Polk who answered.

"That would be best," he assented. "I won't leave

until it's been decided to do something to protect these women."

Hod started for the door and Alamo drifted after him. "While you're gone," Alamo told the other, "I'll just move around and make sure them rips took the hint and pulled out for Tascosa."

There was silence in the ranch kitchen for a long moment following the departure of the pair. The girl broke it to voice an uneasy question. "Polk—are those two men outlaws?"

Polk looked at her sharply. "Why ask that now?" he countered, sparring for time.

"Because they look and act like it," she said at once. "All four of those men plainly knew one another. None of you have ever told us anything about yourselves."

"And maybe I'm an owlhoot too, you mean?" He grinned, more at ease with her than he had ever been.

"*Are* they, Polk?" she pressed.

"They were once, at any rate." It was as far as he would go. Aunty Thankful regarded him with strongly simulated contempt.

"Go 'long with you, boy," she snorted. "They as far out as any outlaw gets—and you know it! But they done right by us. I won't go for to aggravate the good Lord by noticing more than I should," she concluded piously.

He looked at her in faint surprise. Clearly he felt the impulse to tease her mildly. He caught himself, however, and shook his head. "Sam was right," he averred as if to himself. "He swore those boys would stick, and they sure have—so far."

Trinket made clear that she fully intended to trust them after what had happened. "But I'm not at all sure I understand it either." Her brown eyes clouded. "They must know they asked for more trouble today. Those men they recognized came from Tascosa, where they have many friends—"

Burnett nodded. He had got that much. "They'll go

back there," he predicted. "Wonder who this Lasher is they mentioned?"

"I've—heard of him." The girl was distinctly uneasy. "Will he—will they—follow this up, Polk?"

He didn't know. They were still discussing it when hoofs clattered in the yard, and a moment later Hod Lewis and Pat Stevens stepped in, pulling off their hats. Pat had heard what had happened.

"You're all right, I see." His glance flickered to Polk. "Good boy, Burnett. You were smart to figure ahead." It was approval in full, if the puncher had wondered whether he would be asked why he had abandoned the herd without explanation.

"I'm still doing that, Stevens." Polk spoke with a new firmness. "We can't risk a repeat of that kind of business, especially since it was on our account."

"No. Hod mentioned as much." Stevens took the faint reproof calmly. "We'll have to post a watch here at the ranch as long as we're around."

Burnett's hesitation to respond was noticeable, but he watched Pat steadily. The older man glanced toward Trinket.

"Polk did very well," she murmured.

Pat nodded. "I think he did. . . . Then if it's okay with you, Burnett, we'll just leave you posted here to circulate around some and keep your eye peeled."

Polk grunted. "I won't miss much," he promised.

There was more talk before the men left. Burnett sought his pony with the others and rode off alone through the cottonwoods. Trinket understood that she would see little of him, but seemed content to know that he would be on guard. Pat and Hod Lewis returned at once to the big corral, intent on pursuing the hot, dusty work of branding.

That evening nearly the entire crew rode in for supper. From their portentous looks and grave silence it was plain that a conference would be held at the table. Few words were spoken until the meal was nearly over. Then Sam put down his empty coffee cup with a bang. "Any way you look at it," he said, "we've still got better than a day's work ahead of us."

Chuck Skurlock gruffly agreed. "It don't make sense to wait like sitting ducks for them boys in town to come down on us neither."

"What makes you so sure they will?" growled Ezra. He was asking himself if it was smart after all to have hired the owlhoots, since they seemed more likely to attract lightning than avert it.

"Started in already, haven't they?" Hod Lewis said shortly. "I told you Hanlon said something to Miss Martin about harboring us here and mentioned Lasher. To me that means those two weren't acting on their own."

Pat had already arrived at this conclusion. An old hand at fighting fire with fire, he had his answer ready. "We'll have to pick up supplies anyway before we push on," he remarked dryly. "We'll ride into Tascosa with pack ponies in the morning, and kill two birds with one stone."

Alamo gazed at him keenly. "You mean brace Lasher right on his own ground, and face him down?" Whipping the query out in an astonished tone, he paused to weigh the daring proposal. Finally he nodded reluctantly. "That'll do it, Stevens—if you can make it stick. . . . Hang it all, I admire your brass! Something told me it wasn't no mistake to throw in with you."

"It won't work," Jack Utter thrust in gloomily. "But I'll go along anyhow."

"That's right. Me too!" added Lewis.

"No—hold on." Pat held up a hand. "I know you're all hungry for gunsmoke. But we'll do this my way."

"Sure, Stevens. I'll back you up in Tascosa alone!" Alamo grinned.

"This will be a peaceful excursion—we hope. I'm not giving Lasher any excuse for a battle that I know how to avoid. I'll take Skurlock and Sam," Pat stated. "The rest of you will be needed to guard the herd; and Ez will see to it that the branding is pushed along."

There were loud protests, but the men had learned to take Stevens at his word. Trinket Martin expressed her misgivings early the following morning, when the trio prepared to pull out for town. "Hadn't you better take Polk along, just in case?" she asked.

Pat suppressed a smile. "No, we can't be sure you won't need him here," he gave back. "We'll make out."

With Sloan and Chunk, he swung into the saddle a few minutes later. Driving a half dozen docile pack animals, they set off down the creek. Reaching its mouth, they swung east to follow the Canadian, riding under the cottonwoods which shaded the bottoms. The early sun was up, slanting down into the shallow river valley by the time they drew up at the edge of town.

Tascosa boasted of a single wide street with a couple of cross-streets. There were few signs of life at this early hour except for a booted man strolling along some distance from them and a couple of saddled ponies standing at a hitch rail.

As they entered Main Street, however, the town suddenly became alive with men who stepped out of the adobe buildings; there were none who were not armed. The attention of all was stolidly fastened on the new arrivals.

"Must be thirty or forty men here," growled Sam under his breath. "It was a ghost town a few months ago."

Pat only nodded, and Skurlock was equally stoic of manner. "That's McMasters' store yonder, below the Exchange Hotel." He pointed it out.

Men peered out of the hotel doors as they plodded past, and a harsh comment, undecipherable but sardonic, rang out. Glancing ahead, they saw upward of half a dozen rough-looking men in a group on McMasters' store porch.

"That's Lasher there in the middle," Skurlock muttered.

Pat's mouth was a straight, unreadable line. He had

heard of Blue Jaw Lasher and had no trouble in singling the notorious outlaw leader out. Every bit of six feet, with shoulders to match, Lasher revealed a face like blasted granite. Even from a distance of a hundred feet it was possible to make out the old, blue-tinged powder burn which had given him his name, balefully visible through the stubble on his square jaw.

The trio rode forward until only the hitch rack stood between them and the men on the store porch. "Howdy, Blue," Skurlock said, and nodded to the men with Lasher.

Burly and gimlet-eyed, the leader paid no heed to the greeting. "Who are you?" he rasped, surveying Stevens and Sloan grimly.

Sam awkwardly dismounted. "I. M. Stiff," he groaned facetiously in reply.

One or two owlhoots behind Lasher chuckled; others accepted this humorous note with appreciative eye. It appeared to ease the moment's tension somewhat. Then one of Lasher's men stepped down off the single step and moved forward casually. "Welcome, neighbors," he said, as if anxious to help. "I'll take charge of them broncs for you—"

Starting to reach for the reins Sam was looping over the hitch rail, he must have stepped closer than he intended. In a blurred flash of movement Sloan whipped his Colt out. Its barrel cracked audibly against the man's scalp. With a muffled groan, the outlaw wilted and slipped down. Sam coolly stepped back to avoid his writhing legs.

Not a man on the store porch moved so much as a finger. Keenly aware of Stevens and Skurlock sitting their saddles squarely and following all this with hawk-like alertness, they declined to intervene. It was Pat who broke the ominous silence.

"Don't overstep yourself, Lasher. . . . All right, Sam. Lead those pack animals around to the back of the store." Pat's eye rested absently on Lasher while the stocky man did as he was bid. Then Pat inclined his head toward Skurlock. Chunk slipped to the ground and racked his bronc as Sloan had done. He stepped back. Only then did Stevens follow suit, pausing to gaze squarely across the rail at the scowling outlaw leader.

"Since you're curious, we're customers, mister," he spoke coldly. "Driving U. S. Government horses to an army post. Stand away from that door, will you?"

Blue Jaw measured him briefly and made a slight gesture. A lane opened up leading to the open store door. Pat vaulted the rail, while Skurlock unhurriedly passed around its end. Shoulder to shoulder they stepped up on the porch and passed through. If Pat sought out no hostile eye in particular as they brushed close to the bristling owlhoots, neither did he avoid any. The outlaws paid them the grudging compliment of silently falling back without resistance.

Sam had stepped in through the back and was waiting when they entered the store. McMasters was a sallow, mustached man in his late forties who displayed nervous impatience as he turned to wait on them. When Stevens read off a healthy list of wants, he paused, frowning. "I expect you're prepared to pay for all of this?" he queried bluntly.

Pat met his look with one as chilling. "Don't worry. I don't know your custom with others. From me it's cash on the barrelhead—and we don't pay for questions."

Muttering, the merchant turned to fill the order, which under normal circumstances would have inspired him with obsequious alacrity.

9

THE PROPRIETOR'S BUSINESSLIKE air as he filled their order did not altogether cover his eagerness for them to be gone. Sam was busy packing the supplies out the back way and loading the ponies. Stevens paid strict attention to his needs and appeared indifferent to everything else.

Three wooden-faced men had been in the store when they entered. They were obviously owlhoots. Skurlock stood planted in the middle of the floor, dourly eying these men while the others worked.

As if at a signal the three strangers drifted slowly to the front door and stepped out. Skurlock didn't like it. "That bunch will try to stop us when we leave, Stevens," he muttered.

By no means as unaware of his surroundings as he appeared, Pat only nodded. There was no denying that the situation looked bad. Blue Jaw Lasher's heavy voice had been heard rumbling vindictively outside for several minutes, and the group of outlaws on the porch seemed to be growing.

Pat did not let all this distract him from the business at hand. It was not much longer before he checked out the last of their needs. Sloan came in for the final packages, and saw him handing McMasters some bills. "This is it now?" Sam asked quietly. "Keep a record of how much it was, boy. We'll settle up afterward."

His eyes strayed to the front windows as he spoke, and it was not hard to follow his thought. He glanced back to Stevens; their eyes met and Pat nodded significantly. Sam got it. Stepping behind a counter as if

76

to look at a label, a second later he slipped unobtrusively out the back way once more. Hastily he stuffed his bundle under the tarp cover of a pack, then turning toward the street, he skirted the side of the store building and a moment later paused innocently in full view of the wide street.

The owlhoots, who were grouped closely on McMasters' porch, abruptly spotted Sam. When his holster swung around to the front, their muttering broke off and they moved apart.

They had no trouble in divining Sam's object. If it had been their plan to explode into action the minute Stevens and Skurlock emerged from the store, they promptly abandoned it, looking blandly disinterested as the pair appeared. Pat pushed through their midst, pulling his hat forward; Skurlock followed indolently, tossing a jest or two at the men he knew. The owlhoots grinned, keenly appreciating the iron nerve of this trio. It was only Lasher who scowled.

Pat moved out to the street, his brusque movements signifying his taut readiness for anything. Twitching his reins free, he swung astride. "Okay, Sam. Start those pack ponies off."

Getting his own mount, Sloan moved unhurriedly to comply. As the pack animals appeared Skurlock helped keep them in order. Just before starting, Stevens deliberately reined back to face the burly outlaw leader.

"Lasher, keep your men away from Saw Log. That's an order," he let drop curtly.

Hand on hips, Lasher gave him back stare for stare. "Not my responsibility, friend," he tossed back truculently. "Afraid I've no particular control over these boys."

Skurlock raked him with a contemptuous look. "Never mind the lies, Blue. And I can tell you this personally—if Hanlon or Lovat pester those women again—or any of these other jokers you're having so much trouble with—they won't be coming back. Have you got that?"

"I'll pass the word around," said Lasher derisively. "No doubt they'll listen to you, Chunk."

Pat silently waved Skurlock on, and the little pack train moved down the cottonwood-shaded street in what seemed an ominous silence. Skurlock gazed regretfully toward Dunn's Saloon as they plodded by. "Kind of early in the morning, but I sure could use a little tonic." He sighed.

Pat's grin was tight. "Leave well enough alone, Chunk," he said tersely. "I think we froze up the situation here, maybe long enough for us to get away. Just don't crowd your luck."

"It's what you get for nursing government broncs," Skurlock groaned. "I had a hunch it would be this way. I don't pretend to like it."

Not until they were well beyond the edge of town did tension relax. Skurlock looked at Stevens. "Now we're back out of there I got to hand it to you," he confided cheerfully.

Pat's lips twitched. "Why is that, Chunk?"

"First time I ever saw somebody set Lasher back on his heels and make it stick," said Skurlock. "It almost makes me think Blue's got something up his sleeve—"

Pat shrugged. "He knows what to expect if he makes a pass at us. At least it'll give us a little time. The thing to do now is to get back to the herd and push that branding hard."

Although the time in Tascosa had seemed long, they were back at the Saw Log well before noon. Sloan delayed at the ranch to stow the fresh supplies in the camp wagon while Pat and Skurlock pushed on out to the work corral. The men knocked off briefly at their appearance, curiosity on their bronzed faces.

"Made it to town and back, eh?" Alamo accosted Pat. "Hope you picked up my tobacco. Did you—run into any trouble?"

Tossing over a sack of makings, Pat shook his head. "We ran into Lasher, if that's what you mean. We gave him to understand what we were there for, and I think he got it all right."

Alamo, looking astonished, glanced toward Skurlock suspiciously. "You mean he let you fellows ride back out of there, just like that?"

Pat's nod was even briefer. The outlaws glanced at one another. "You want to bet it don't end there?" Hod Lewis threw out hardily.

"That's right. You ain't got Lasher figured, Stevens, if you think that," added Jack Utter.

Pat disposed of the prediction with an impatient wave. "We pulled up here to get those roans branded," he said. "Shall we get about it?"

They turned back to the task without more talk, and although searching glances were tossed toward the open range from time to time, it was plain now that all were anxious to get the job over and done. As it developed, the dark expectations of the owlhoots proved not without foundation. During the afternoon a lone rider jogged up the creek, approached the corral boldly, and drew rein to watch the proceedings. Within ten minutes he was joined by a second man.

Helping to cut out the roans, run them up to the fire and rope and throw the animals for branding, Stevens found occasion to shove his pony up alongside of Alamo. "Acquaintances of yours?" He jerked his head toward the newcomers.

Alamo nodded grimly. "They're both from Tascosa," he said. "They got their gall showing up here as bold as brass!"

Pat failed to register concern. "They figure the boys know them, I suppose."

It was true enough. In the course of half an hour several others joined the first arrivals. Clearly their interest was casual. They clung in a loose group at the unoccupied side of the corral. A few climbed the bars to perch on top; others rested elbows on the rail, watching; and they kept up a running fire of jests among themselves. It was not long before one called out facetiously to Skurlock, who missed a cast at a frisky roan. In a matter of minutes the air was full of banter.

Chunk and Hod Lewis answered the jibes in kind, glancing warily toward Stevens and Ezra to see how they were taking it. Sam was not above cracking a joke or two of his own. The laughter was uproarious when he invited the newcomers to pitch in and help.

"When I'm caught burning the US iron on a good horse," one sang out, "you can mark me down for crazy."

There were even more pointed quips, to all of which the working owlhoots responded with good humor. Pat recognized their finesse in refusing to take offense at anything. But running a fresh batch of horses into the corral, young Burnett put on a face of iron at the remarks flying about. He shook his head reprovingly at Pat's calm wink.

"You're making a big mistake, Stevens," warned the puncher. "You must know those buzzards have gathered here for no good. Let them get chummy with our boys, and the fat will be in the fire."

Pat looked at him shrewdly. "How come you're out here, instead of at the ranch?"

"Sam said he'd keep an eye open." Polk was sternly resolute. "Want to get this job done, don't we?"

Pat nodded. "You're right there."

"Then why don't you send those birds packing?" snapped Burnett. "They're just a damned nuisance, holding up the work!"

To his surprise Stevens promptly demurred. "Unh-uh. They don't hold us up that much. Start something now, and it's just asking for complications."

"You were warned—" began Polk.

Pat cut him off with crisp decision. "Did you spot any of these hardcases hanging around the Saw Log?"

Burnett shook his head. "Not yet."

Pat grunted. "That's still your job, boy. You can let me worry about things here."

Polk subsided, but it was typical of his youth and inexperience of men that he could not let the matter drop. The Tascosa crowd was still hanging about later in the afternoon, but showing signs of getting ready to pull away, when Burnett again sought out Pat. This time his manner was portentous.

"Stevens, did you know Jack Utter is gone?" he whipped out.

Calmly verifying the fact before he spoke, the older man nodded. "He is at that. Could be he's on some errand or other to the wagon. Did you see him go?"

Polk said, "No. And I don't believe anyone else did." His look was accusing. "You're just asking for desertions here. How sure are you these roughs from Tascosa had nothing to do with it?"

Pat frowned this down. "Utter's a grown man, Burnett," he gave back bluntly. "He should know how to look after himself. If he can't it's his hard luck."

Aware that he could get nowhere with this man, Polk gave up with poorly suppressed exasperation. However, Stevens did not forget Utter's unexplained absence. The loss of even a single man made a difference, and by the time dusk settled over the range, putting an end to activities for that day, there remained still a couple of hours' work which must be finished up on the morrow.

If no one seemed aware of exactly when he put in an appearance, Utter was with the others, vastly innocent and casual of manner, when they stamped into the Saw Log kitchen for supper. Stevens coolly called Jack to account before the men. "This is hardly the time to ride off on your own chores, Utter. Where were you?"

Jack pretended surprise. "Who, me?"

"You rode over to Tascosa on your own, didn't you? What were you doing there?"

"Well, I traded lead with one of Lasher's boys, for one thing, Stevens, and I'm afraid he lost," Utter gave back, embarrassed but stanch. "I'm counting on you to stick by me," he added frankly.

The other owlhoots stared at him. "You shot one of Blue's hands, Utter? . . . Who was it?" Skurlock thrust in harshly.

"It happened to be Bat Hanlon. But it wasn't my

fault, Stevens. Hanlon asked for it!" he protested stoutly.

"Give us the rest of it," directed Pat.

Utter paused. "Why, I rode in to smell out the ground—you know how it is. I ran into Hanlon in the Exchange Bar. Bat offered me a drink, and I went along with that. Pretty soon he started hinting around. I caught on that some scheme was cooking and Hanlon wanted me in on it."

"Yes. And—?" Pat would not let up on him.

"Well, I find out Bat and a few of the boys were planning to stampede the roans when we least expected it. That's why some of them were out here this afternoon to look the deal over. It made me mad."

Pat's lips were tight. "So what happened?"

"I corked him smack in the chops, Stevens. Bat went down flat. Then I seen him snatch his gun out. . . . I beat him to it," ended Jack simply.

"So what was the result of that?"

"Nothing much. There were a couple of Blue's boys in the bar. They kept their hands away from their guns while I got out of there fast."

"And the upshot is that you killed Hanlon, and Lasher knows who and where you are," said Pat evenly. His headshake was dour. "If you ask me, Utter, the whole thing was royally stupid! You had no choice once you got into it," he conceded. "But did you *have* to go to Tascosa?"

"Why hang it all!" Jack was vehement, the angry blood darkening his craggy visage. "Able to tip you off to a dirty deal, wasn't I? That stampede would have hit us without no warning at all."

"I can say one thing," Pat answered curtly. "Whether it would have come or not, you've made it certain now. . . . Well, you stuck with us, Utter, and we're ready to stick with you now. But from now on do as you're told. The whole trouble with the pack of you is that you're trying to do our thinking for us!"

Hod Lewis started up from the table resentfully. "Give us our orders, then."

"You can go on out to the herd right now, Lewis, and relieve old Kip," Pat threw back. "We know what to expect. The only question is how long Lasher will wait before he moves."

Hod looked regretfully at his half-finished meal. "Dang you, Jack—" he growled at Utter. Sam's chuckle over his discomfiture thawed the scowling stiffness of the others. They watched Lewis turn outside without delay, his action somehow symbolizing their collective loyalty.

"What about us, Stevens?" Alamo asked.

"Pile that grub into you and get going," returned Pat briefly. "We'll stand a full watch tonight. It's my guess Lasher will be so hot he'll strike in a hurry. If we can block his game we will stand a chance."

Silence fell as the heavy dishes and tin cups were plied with a will. Even the women spoke in hushed tones, aware of the gravity of the situation. It was only a matter of minutes before the men stood up from the table, ready to shuffle out. Pat led the way to the yard. "Utter, you can stay here with Burnett and watch the ranch and the camp wagon," he instructed. "Lasher will be looking for you out there. I don't want any more killings."

Jack grunted. For once, however, he put up no argument. Swinging astride his bronc, he threw a glance toward Polk. "We'll make a circle of the flat right off," he said. "You go that way."

As the pair jogged off into the dusk, Ezra turned to Pat. "Let's get organized, Stevens," he proposed gruffly. "We might as well all know what we have to do."

"We'll run the roans into the big corral and hold them there," said Pat promptly. "That's the first thing. What comes after, we'll see."

Sam made a sensible proposal or two, and they were still discussing it briefly, their ponies stamping in the yard, when two shots close together rent the thickening darkness under the cottonwoods farther along the creek. A second later Jack Utter's aroused yell drifted to them.

A couple of Saw Log storage sheds had been built down by the creek some distance from the house. It was from there that the shots had sounded. Turning that way, the crew abruptly made out an ominous red glow against the sky. Polk Burnett came pounding into the yard while they stared.

"Look alive, Stevens!" the puncher cried. "Lasher's crowd has fired one of the sheds! Utter thought he saw somebody running. There's still a chance we can grab the skunk that did it!"

10

SEVERAL HANDS STARTED precipitately in the direction of the blaze. Pat's angry blast headed them off. "Forget that fire," he hurled at them. "It's just bait. Pile out to the work corral fast. You'll find your work cut out for you!"

Their ponies swept away toward the open range. In only a couple of minutes they were within dim and distant sight of the corral. Faint cries and the flat bang of a shot reached them.

"It's a raid," cried Sam wrathfully, ramming his mount forward at breakneck speed. "We'll be lucky if we save Lewis and old Kip—!"

Red flashes stabbed the gloom out on the range. It was just possible to make out the dark shape of the corral and the milling horse herd. Despite a slashing attack by an unknown number of men the guards were putting up a hot defense.

"Spread out," called Stevens. "Mop up anybody you come across!"

They swept close to the corral on a dead run. Guns were still banging; the fire seemed to be concentrated at a point near the opposite side of the big pen. A big-framed figure was racing around the corral fence, yelping ferociously. Pat made out Hod Lewis' harsh tones.

"What goes on, Lewis?" he called.

"Bunch of rowdies trying to rip the bars down," Hod threw back. "They're aiming to stampede the stuff, Stevens!"

The aroused crew gathered around the wide curve of the pen. A blast of scattered gunfire met them from the far side. A few answered, but Pat held off until he learned where old Kip James might be.

A fierce screech informed him only a moment later. Three attackers were trying to tear down the side of the corral, wrenching at the stout poles while the plucky old rawhide dived into them like a wildcat. Cursing could be heard and the sharp struggle swayed this way and that.

"Kip's in the middle of that hassle," sang out Alamo. "Looks like they're figuring to drag him off."

He and Sloan rammed their broncs straight into the melee, slashing right and left with their pistol barrels. A big man turned in the saddle, blasting a shot off almost under Sam's nose.

"Is that you, Lasher?" Sam rasped harshly. "Here's a present for you!" His own Colt crashed, and the other's form swiftly faded into the darkness.

Other raiders were pulling away as speedily as possible, with the weight of numbers now clearly against them. A man on a dancing horse tried to throw an arm around the wiry Kip, hoisting him up bodily in the attempt to abduct him. Old James kicked out with his spurs, and the rider's mount pitched wildly, threatening at any second to throw him. With a snarl the fellow flung Kip sprawling in the dust and wheeled away.

A second afterward hoofs drummed a staccato rhythm as the attackers drew off. A blast of gunfire followed them. Some took time to throw lead backward over their shoulders, but fortunately no one was hit.

Moments before, seeing how matters stood, Stevens had hurled himself straight for the gap in the corral, where the raiders had succeeded in ripping out the best part of the panel or two. Pat yelled at Utter, waving him that way. "We've got to block this hole" he cried above the pound of guns. "If the roans spook and break out, those blacklegs will have the stampede they played for!"

Jack got the point fast. Taking a stand in the opening, he yelled for the others. "Hod! Alamo! Where the hell are you all?

Hod Lewis heard and so did Ezra. It was the latter who sized up the situation in a twinkling. He whipped a rope off his saddle-horn. "Grab this," he yelled at Lewis. "We'll run it across the break fast!"

Within a matter of seconds they had stout rope barring the opening in the corral. Hod quickly knotted his end on an upright, and Ez as speedily ran a second strand across lower down. They were none too soon. Already the alarmed roans were churning and stamping about the broad corral. Ez was yanking his second strand taut when a lunging equine body slammed into the ropes. Another followed. Pat and the others quelled this flurry, slapping at the tossing heads of the horses with their hats.

Once away from the corral, the Tascosa raiders did not flee far. Scattering in the gloom and setting up a harassing fire from a distance, they constantly moved about. Firing a hot return, Sloan yelled scathing epithets at them. It was impossible, however, to goad them into a fresh attack. "Shall we drive these buggers off, Stevens?" demanded Sam fiercely.

"No, leave it alone." Pat's flat tone was a warning. "They came mighty close to scattering the herd as it is. They tried to draw us off with that shed fire, and they'd like nothing better now."

At his direction the gap in the corral was effectively

stopped, and the men were posted in a scattered line around the corral. Once they ceased their random fire, the renegades likewise gradually slacked off, though they continued to pour slugs in from time to time. Occasionally one ricocheted off a corral pole, and Pat was concerned lest a horse or two might be struck; but none had as yet gone down.

"Better count noses here, after that brush" Pat told Sam.

Assenting, the stocky man jogged off around the corral. "All accounted for, boy," he reported on his return. "Utter got a crease across his shoulder, but that's all—"

"Jack did? I expected that—and Utter should have," returned Pat. "They were laying for him. No question that Bat Hanlon has friends in that Tascosa crowd."

"We broke this up" said Sam thoughtfully. "What now? Will they come at us again?"

Pat didn't bother to hazard a guess. "It means an all-night watch. We'll wind up the branding in the morning. Then we're on our way."

"That'll be a danged relief" grunted Sam.

As they talked, the other hands rode at a quiet drifting pace around the corral. Chunk Skurlock heard the exchange as he passed and reined back for a word.

"If you're smart, Stevens, you'll figure to circle Tascosa real wide and make distance fast," he advised gruffly.

Before Pat could reply another voice thrust in. "You're not talking about pulling away from here and leaving those women completely unprotected, I hope!" Polk Burnett rode close out of the gloom. "You can't do that, Stevens!"

The question had already presented itself to Pat's mind. He had no definite answer ready. "We haven't done that yet, Burnett," he returned coolly. "Something will be worked out." To distract the other from his deep concern he changed the subject abruptly. "Better get back to Saw Log now, hadn't you, and see how that fire is doing? Take old Kip along. And you both better stand a watch right there at the ranch to-night."

Polk was more than ready to run the risk of a return to the ranch through the darkness. The red glow which had stained the sky for some time in that direction was slowly dying out. He turned away to locate the cook, and Skurlock pursued his vigil with the others.

For better than two hours the frustrated raiders continued to fire sporadically from the gloom-enfolded range. They did not offer to return to the attack after a futile sortie or two; and since their ineffectual harassment was largely ignored, it finally died away.

The star-shot night seemed long. The men were still maintaining a careful watch by the time the first faint streaks of dawn paled the eastern sky. Stevens declared that in another hour half of them would ride in for breakfast. At their return the rest would follow.

Weary as they were, not a man suggested delaying the completion of the branding. But Alamo's remark to Stevens on their way in to eat made it plain that all minds were busy. "This is a scrubby setup," the owl-hoot said. "Once we pull out of here, Stevens, them ornery pups in town will either hound the women here on Saw Log—or else they'll dog us clear to the Little Colorado!"

Pat made no attempt to minimize the looming threat. "I'm afraid you're right, Alamo. I'll talk it over with Ezra and we'll come up with something."

What the lanky one-eyed Bar ES partner came up with when the subject was broached to him was a snort of wrath. "We'll have to polish off that smart Lasher before we get done with him," he predicted grimly. "Might as well do it now!"

Pat was not ready to go that far. "I'll tell you what though" he said, catching the other's eye with a steady look. "You and I will shove on into town right now, Ez. We may be able to toss a scare into that hombre that will tighten things up enough for us to get away."

Ezra was profanely willing to try anything that promised action. Done eating, they got up their mounts without further talk and set off quietly down Cheyenne Creek. On watch at the ranch, Polk Burnett saw them start out. About to pound after them, he took a second sharp look and checked his horse. Something in their purposeful mien warned the puncher they were in no mood for delay.

Both riders matter-of-factly checked their guns as they neared Tascosa. Ez spun his cylinder with a thumb and glanced up. "Expect you know what we might be riding into here—"

"You mean after last night." Pat's tone was unruffled. "If I thought this crowd was even loosely organized, Ez, I'd think twice about showing myself here at all. But these owlhoots are pretty much on their own —or they think they are. They'll stick with Lasher, or any other leader, just as long as he proves himself to be the big boss."

Ezra weighed this without further comment. He had watched Stevens in action before and knew what it spelled. Slapping his black flatbrim down over his face, he sat straighter in the saddle.

Riding into town knee to knee, they watched alertly for any sign of treachery. Tascosa was already stirring with subdued activity this morning. Men saw them coming; a few froze, staring; others ducked quickly from sight, and these, Pat could only conclude, knew more about last night's raid than they should and were wary of retaliation.

There was no concerted effort to block the progress of the pair, and this was a favorable sign. It was equally clear that no concessions were to be made when a rocky-visaged man moved across the street on foot directly in their path. Pat coolly reined in, blocking the fellow.

"Where would I find Lasher, neighbor?"

"You might look most anywheres." The man's beady eyes flashed defiance. "If you *really* want him it won't be necessary to look far."

These words told Stevens that his visit was no surprise, and that more than a few of the outlaws were holding themselves in check while awaiting the outcome. Pat shrugged, glancing at Ez and jerking his chin toward the squat, adode brick Exchange Hotel.

"We'll start there."

Racking their broncs under an overshadowing cottonwood, they moved quietly toward the entrance to the bar. Pat walked in first; he had barely entered before his eye fell on a shadowy group of four or five men in low-voiced conclave well to the rear of the place. He spotted Blue Jaw Lasher among the others. As the man who was talking to Lasher turned, Pat's nerves tightened. He recognized Hook Larsen instantly.

Larsen's appearance in Tascosa could mean only one thing: that the Colorado railroad war had collapsed, for this season at least, and Hook's daredevil gunfighters were on the prowl. Larsen would have lost no time explaining his grudge against Stevens to Lasher. Whether or not this was the cause of last night's determined attack on the Bar ES herd, it boded no good for the future. Pat did not need to be warned that only bold self-confidence could extricate them from the hornet's nest into which they had walked.

He halted in the middle of the saloon floor, hands on hips. "There you are, Lasher. Who said you were hard to find?"

The outlaw leader blustered forward with ominous authority. "Let's hope you're not sorry you did," he snarled.

"I guess not." Pat drawled. "In a pinch I'd have followed a lot farther—after you pulled that stupid trick last night."

Lasher tightened up in a flash. "What trick?" He stepped still closer, his choleric jaw thrust out. "Be mighty careful who you're accusing, Stev—"

His savage utterance broke off abruptly as Pat's iron fist caught him flush on the button. Arms flying, Lasher went over backward with a crash.

On the instant, moving smoothly aside, Ezra showed the watching owlhoots the business end of his ready

Colt. If they pretended to ignore Ez, hooting at Stevens and calling out, there was no rush to overwhelm him, nor were guns drawn. "Don't take it from him, Blue!" a man urged harshly. "Get up and stomp him down!"

Still lying there, half supported on one elbow, Lasher had no intention of taking this advice. Suddenly his free arm jerked as he sought to yank out his weapon. Pat was too far away to flatten him with a boot, but his kick at Lasher's extended legs jarred the outlaw so that his gun bounced out on the floor beside him. Before he could pounce on it, Pat's own gun crashed. It sent Lasher's Colt leaping away.

Pat straightened, measuring the cringing owlhoot with icy eyes. "Some people never learn. That's the way Bat Hanlon asked for his—if you've forgotten already."

Pat's words gave the hulking outlaw pause. He held himself motionless. "I'm not forgetting Hanlon, and be damned to you!" he cried harshly.

"I'm apt to remember a few things too," retorted Pat coolly. "And so will Utter. You were seen out there at our corral, Lasher, no matter what you tell these birds!"

"You're a liar! I never—"

Pat's boot flew up again, catching Lasher on the point of the shoulder as he sought to struggle up and tumbling him back ignominiously. "Here's something else you be sure to remember. We're pulling out today. Lift a hand to make trouble for us and, Lasher, I'll come back for your hide. Do you savvy that?"

Lasher's eyes blazed his impotent fury but he got no words out, his breath audibly rasping. Pat swept his confederates with a stern look. "That goes for all of you busy characters," he snapped. "Pass the word around—or get ready to fight the buzz saw!"

There was no answer. Pat glanced at Ezra. "Nothing else to hold us here," he muttered.

Ez waited until Pat had coolly turned his back and strode out, then he backed out in his wake. A few men came running along the street as they swung astride, but there was something about this grimly self-possessed pair which kept the taut situation from exploding into violence.

Deliberately they turned their ponies and started off. Not until they were well beyond earshot did Ezra speak. "You sure cut it mighty fine, boy. I thought for a minute there we had a battle on our hands."

Pat chuckled. "So did I," he confided. "But it was the only way, Ez. Run from that crowd, and they'll be on your back in a flash."

Safely out of town, they lost no time in striking out for Saw Log. All was quiet at the ranch, but they met Alamo hurrying in from the work corral just as they arrived.

"Where you been, Stevens?" the owlhoot cried. "We're washed up with the branding out there and ready to drag it—" He broke off, noting their sober faces. "Holy smoke! You ain't been to Tascosa again?"

Young Polk and Trinket heard their talk from across the yard. "Oh!" the girl exclaimed tensely. "I was afraid of this! What happened, Pat?"

Burnett allowed no time for Pat's answer. "Trink—no matter what it was, it's bad! Pack up the wagon," he urged her, "and come along with us to Matagorda. It's the only way out for you now. We can't leave you behind to face those wolves alone!"

11

TRINKET LOOKED TOWARD Pat, who read the deep concern she sought to hide. "Surely you don't think there's real danger for us—?"

"You lost a shed already," Polk reminded her, befor Pat could speak. "Come away for a few weeks and this business will blow over. Those outlaws will drift away before you get back, and it'll be safe."

But the girl still waited for Pat to respond. Faced with her dilemma, he shook his head. "Once we leave you here I can't promise a thing," he admitted candidly. "Lasher's crowd have already shown their teeth."

"But we'll be in your way," protested Trinket uncertainly.

Aunty Thankful had appeared in the kitchen doorway moments ago, listening to this talk with thinly pursed lips. It was she who made the final decision, taking charge firmly. "You, Alamo man," she barked, stabbing a finger at him. "Hitch up our ranch wagon right off, you hear? If you men are going away from here *I* ain't staying, nor Trink neither. . . . Get your clothes packed, girl."

Trinket still looked toward Pat, who grinned faintly. "You better do as she says," he murmured. "She's the boss."

Trinket waited for no more and hurried into the house. Stevens hastily instructed old Kip to get the camp wagon ready to move out and then thrust on to the work corral. There he found Sloan ready and chafing to be off.

"Branding all done, eh?" Pat asked him.

"All washed up. And man, if we don't take the edge off these roans with a little travel, there won't be no holding 'em."

Taking a rough count to make sure no material loss had been sustained, Ezra gave the sign for the herd to get under way. Bunching them, they started the horses south. As they neared Saw Log, old Kip appeared driving the cook wagon. Behind it came the ranch rig with several battered trunks roped at the back. Trinket was on the seat, and beside her, straight as a ramrod and wearing a flowered hat, Aunty Thankful handled the reins.

Pat rode toward them to call out directions. "Better fall back and trail behind us today," he directed Kip. "The women will stay with you."

As the cavalcade set off, Pat rode on ahead to the point, where he conferred with Ezra. Sam noted the course they were taking: it looked precisely as if the intention was to drive straight through Tascosa. He kept his own counsel, however.

Young Burnett noticed also. He shoved forward to accost Pat. "Stevens, have you forgot the US brand on these broncs?" he demanded. "Pushing them right through town is certain to bring on an uproar!"

Pat surveyed him mildly. "Think so?" His tone was unconcerned. "We really haven't much choice, boy. Tascosa is the only decent stock crossing on the Canadian for fifty or sixty miles in either direction."

Even Trinket seemed doubtful of Pat's wisdom when he dropped back later to assure himself the wagons were in order. The direction they were taking was not lost on the girl. "I hope you're not making a mistake," she told him plainly.

He smiled at her. "I don't think so."

Hod Lewis, riding in the drag, must have understood how the women felt. He turned in the saddle to look back. "You've got brass, Stevens," he said admiringly. "It's the only thing that will get you out of this."

Pat waved him back to his work. "I'm counting on

you fellows, Lewis. It's not only *my* gall that'll do the trick, believe me."

He pushed forward again, helping Chunk Skurlock to quell an outbreak among the roans and lining them out afresh. The near approach to town found him about midway of the strung-out herd. Up at the point, Ezra and Alamo headed the drive straight into Tascosa's Main Street.

There was a ceaseless clatter and scrape of hoofs under the cottonwoods lining the length of the street. The roans had barely reached the edge of town when men came running out to look. Obviously the sight filled these owlhoots with deep astonishment. Their jaws dropped. Blue Jaw Lasher had passed the word around that Stevens would be moving out today, but it had never entered their heads that the intrepid Powder Valley men might come this way, brashly and without any attempt at concealment.

Riding near the head of the drive, Jack Utter boldly waved to an acquaintance or two. The hard-faced outlaws jerked an involuntary acknowledgment and seemed about to swallow their tobacco. They gaped as their eyes fell on the big, unmistakable US government brand, freshly burned on the sleek roan flanks. Clearly such barefaced effrontery was new in their experience.

As the nervous roans thundered down the street, Pat pressed forward watchfully while Sam guarded the opposite side. Both were on the alert, certain some disturbance or other was bound to erupt before they could clear the town. Wherever they were not busy crowding the broncs back into line, their watchful gaze raked the faces of every strange man on the store porches, in livery gangways, or grouped behind the hitch racks.

It was already clear to Stevens that no concerted reception had been planned in Tascosa. From the number of saddled ponies standing ready, he surmised that a number of outlaws at least had expected to sally forth this morning in search of the drive. If this were the case, a strategy meeting might well be in progress somewhere. He kept a sharp lookout for the first glimpse of Hook Larsen or Lasher.

The lead roans were passing Ryan's Saloon when a racket suddenly broke out inside the bar. Several men could be heard yelling and cursing. A gun thudded hollowly inside. Almost at once eight or ten big-hatted figures tumbled out through the front door. Snatching out their six guns, they fired at random, creating a wild uproar.

Pat rushed to master the half-crazed horses. He knew the whole affair was deliberate. It also crossed his mind that if the drovers attempted to retaliate it might well be the end of the drive. Seeing Jack Utter loom close through the roiling dust which clouded the entire street, Stevens rammed his pony around, crowding between the wrathful owlhoot and his erstwhile pals.

"Blast it, Stevens! Get out of my way—" cried Utter tightly.

"Never mind. Get on with your work, Jack." Pat snapped the order at him.

His meaning seemed to dawn on Utter, who jerked an abashed nod and whirled away. There was need for their every effort as the uproar swelled. The Tascosa rowdies all but shot under the heels of the roans, all the while pretending to be desperately engrossed in their own fight.

It was touch and go to keep the herd from stampeding. Somehow the hands rammed it past the point of disturbance without a direct clash between themselves and the rioters. Laboring mightily in the drag, Polk Burnett realized suddenly that the wagons were directly behind and that Trinket Martin would be exposed to this wild outburst of gunfire.

Before he could act, however, Aunty Thankful took matters into her own capable hands. Seeing what was afoot, the slight, elderly woman surged up out of the wagon seat, a huge scattergun in her skinny hands.

She threw it up boldly and blazed away point-blank at the skirmishing outlaws, the gun making a tremendous roar. Its load took effect too. Several owlhoots straightened up with a jerk, clapping hands to various parts of their anatomy with squalls of pain and fury.

Despite Trinket's protestations, Aunty Thankful gave the renegades no time for meditation. The scattergun leveled afresh, and once more its thunderous crash rent the air. The rioters gave up forthwith, flying in a dozen directions and scrambling madly for cover while the mirthful whoops of their more fortunate companions applauded the old colored woman's marksmanship and spunk.

"Git out of here, you no good rapscallions, you!" she screamed fiercely, waving the empty gun in defiance. "Show your worthless faces again and I'll give you another dose. I won't stand for no claptrap from the likes of such trash. You hear me?"

Pat had reined sharply back at the first clap of the scattergun, fearful of what it might portend. Through the swirling dust he glimpsed Trinket's determined guardian in action. The raucous laughter of the discomfited owlhoots told him how they were taking it, and he silently blessed the courageous woman. Make a hard-boiled range warrior laugh and you have drawn his fangs. Perhaps nothing else could have averted serious trouble.

"Hey, Stevens!" called Sam from the far edge of the herd. When Pat looked that way Sam thumbed ahead significantly. He had no time for more as several spooked roans sought to break down a cross-street. He and Hod Lewis vented harsh cowboy yelps and raced after the rebels to turn them.

Pat worked up along the nervous horses, peering through the golden pall of haze swirling under the cottonwoods. On the hotel corner he spotted three or four men standing motionless in the open and watching the drive with baleful interest. Hook Larsen's big, rawboned frame was easy to pick out. Blue Jaw was with him. Pat did not recognize the others.

Pat delayed to face the outlaw leaders squarely for the space of a second or two, returning their brazen stares expressionlessly. No word was uttered on either side, but Pat saw Larsen's eyes slide wickedly over the US brand and then slant back to take in the following wagons.

If Ezra, Alamo and the others at the point had taken note of Lasher and his confederates, they paid no heed, urging the roans on toward the shallow ford of the Canadian beyond the edge of town.

The panic caused by the outbreak of gunfire had been barely weathered without disaster. Rushing at the ford, the roans churned and splashed across; the men yelled and waved ropes and hats on each flank to keep them straightened out. When the last broncs clambered dripping out on the far side, Pat gave a gusty sigh of satisfaction. Once on the southern bank the roans appeared to release fresh energy, dashing wildly on to put behind them the fright experienced in Tascosa. Glancing back, Stevens saw that as yet none of the outlaws were making an effort to follow.

The cook wagon and the Saw Log rig canted down over the north bank and lurched across the shallow stream, with the teams being frantically urged forward to prevent their miring. Polk Burnett had hauled up at the crossing to help in case the wagons got into trouble. Satisfying himself of this, Pat spurred on after the drive.

The herd clattered out of the willow-tangled bottoms between low swells of range land, and the famed Canadian was nearly a mile to the rear before the horses displayed a willingness to calm down. The hands called back and forth to one another jubilantly, applauding the astonishing success of the bold experiment of ramming the roans straight through Tascosa. They cracked jokes and grinned triumphantly in Pat's direction. His stock was high with them at the moment.

"We made it, Ez," Stevens commented tersely, riding up beside the Lanky Bar ES partner.

Ezra's answer was a grunt. He had never been one to enthuse much before all the cards were down. Demonstrating that his single eye did not miss much, he opened up on another subject altogether. "The boys did pretty well," he said. "But I expect you already noticed that Jack Utter got lost in the shuffle—"

Pat glanced about quickly. "No, I didn't." It was not a complete surprise to him, yet he seemed inclined to shrug it off. "Skurlock or one of the others must know what Jack is up to," he said after a moment.

But Chunk did not. "Utter never told me a thing, Stevens," he said flatly. "I don't keep tabs on the boys and it's news to me that he's gone." His expression told that he didn't think much of the idea either.

When Pat put the same question to Alamo, he whipped out, "Utter gone? Ain't a bit surprised. That fool has been begging for grief, and he nearly got it after he tangled with Hanlon. Better slap him down hard, Stevens, if you expect Jack to finish the drive."

Pat's eyes narrowed at this evidence of disagreement among the owlhoots. "If I know what you're thinking, I won't believe it till I'm dead sure," he gave back levelly. "Utter's reckless, but I'll give him credit so far for playing a straight deck."

The sandy-haired little outlaw was impatient. "He could be figuring on that too. You're not out of the woods yet," he reminded Pat.

Pat dropped the matter there. But later he went to the length of questioning old Kip James. "Did you happen to see Utter turn back there in Tascosa, Kip?"

The testy rawhide shook his head. "He was with us across the Canadian," he declared. "He faded into them willows on the flats, and I thought he was up ahead—"

Weighing this, Pat kept his own counsel until the waning afternoon bade them pull up. Utilizing a rock-walled arroyo in which to hold the stock while all hands enjoyed a hearty meal, they were waiting for old Kip's irascible hail when the missing owlhoot rode unobtrusively into camp, striving to act as if he hoped he had not been missed. His fellow outlaws stared at him angrily.

"Where in hell you been?" Alamo demanded point-blank.

"Working—just like you, I hope." Jack sought to turn the question off facetiously.

Busy at the rope corral, Sam Sloan caught a part of this talk and came forward. His eyes fell on Utter, and his broad jowls went rigid with disapproval. "You back, Utter? Give an account of yourself."

Jack looked incredulous. "Me?" he barked. "Why, you saw Hook Larsen there in Tascosa, Sloan! Don't tell a man you didn't get what that means—"

"What does it mean?" Sam broke in on his tirade incisively.

"It means he'll follow us, that's what," Utter hurled out with vigor.

"So what did you do about it?"

"Once we got clear of town I laid back and watched the trail for a good two hours." Jack met Sam's accusing gaze squarely. "Now go ahead and tell me that wasn't good sense!"

Not altogether persuaded, Sam studied the man stonily. "And what did you see?"

"Not a thing." The owlhoot spread his horny palms. "I can't figure it out, Sloan. I told you the scheme Bat Hanlon spilled. . . . But not a single rider came after us that I was able to spot."

"So you rode on to tell us. *Is that all,* Utter?" Sam shot at him.

"Sure it's all," Jack swore vehemently. "I see now I should've told Stevens or somebody. But there wasn't hardly time."

There was more talk, Alamo and the others making plain their opinion of such actions. Stevens heard most of it, but chose to remain in the background. Admitting to himself that Utter put a good face on his unexplained absence, he reserved final judgment, having kept his fingers crossed where these owlhoots were concerned from the first.

Well aware the men were touchy and independent, it was Pat's instinct to let well enough alone until treachery was proven. He would have let the matter ride had not Hod Lewis come to him for a word in private after supper.

"Stevens, I don't like to hand this to you. But Jack Utter always was thick with Lasher's crowd," said Lewis plainly. "I happen to know he was hobnobbing with them boys in Tascosa—and it wasn't just Bat Hanlon either."

Pat weighed this intelligence deliberately. It tallied with his own impression, and he nodded. "Do you think Utter intends to quit the drive, Lewis? Or maybe hand us a fast double cross?"

Hod's rugged face was stolid and expressionless. "That I don't know."

Pat shrugged and turned. "Then we'll find out. Come along, and we'll have a talk with Utter." He set off with purposeful stride.

12

UTTER WAS ROLLING a smoke after his supper when Pat and Hod Lewis advanced toward him. Jack started to turn away absently, but Stevens halted him.

"Jack."

Licking his cigarette paper, Utter glanced sidewise with an air of innocence. Pat came to a halt within two feet of him. "Utter, I've been told you're pretty thick with Lasher's men."

"What's that? Who's been lying about me?" the owl-hoot blustered angrily.

Pat slapped the cigarette out of his mouth with a

lightning cuff, which swept Utter's feet out from under him. Jack went down jarringly, a yell escaping him. His Colt bounced out of the scabbard a second before his hand slapped the empty leather. Pat coolly put his foot down on the gun. Rolling over on his back, propped up on his elbows, Utter glared in outrage.

"What's the meaning of this?" he ripped out.

Although Pat was operating under a head of steam, his tone maintained the same steady level. "Never mind the smoke screen, friend. Will you talk now, or later?"

With savage imprecations, Utter thrashed over on his knees and endeavored to struggle up. Stevens calmly reached down, grasped one of his boots and gave it a vigorous twist. Again Jack sprawled full-length, banging his head smartly.

"Let me up, blast it!" he bawled. He tried to crawl backward, half sitting up. Pat crowded close remorselessly, his fist poised a couple of feet from the outlaw's quivering jaw.

"Give it up, Utter," he advised tightly.

Jack abruptly raised a hand in bewildered surrender. "Okay, Stevens," he growled. "I'm not afraid of you or a dozen like you—but you got me all wrong!"

"I'll be the judge of that. Why did you go back to Tascosa?" Pat rapped compellingly.

Rubbing his jaw, Utter slowly rose. "I did shove on back to town," he confessed. "If there's friends of mine in Tascosa, what's it to you?"

Pat nodded unemotionally. "That's right. You were there before too. Maybe you'd like to stay with your friends."

"Hell no." Jack was vehement. "It ain't healthy for me there, Stevens." For the first time he showed alarm.

"How's that?"

"I went back to talk a pal into pulling out, and I ran into Lasher. He tried to make a deal with me to double cross you and Ezra and Sloan. I turned him down flat."

"Why?" Pat asked bluntly.

"Hang it all, you sold me on getting into the cavalry," Jack said in exasperation. "I want to do that, Stevens—and these roans will do the trick if anything will! With women along like this, those army officers won't be so suspicious." He sounded deeply offended now. "Lasher got nasty when I threw him down. I had to duck lead to get out of Tascosa. And this is the thanks I get!"

"Is that all?" Pat pressed unremittingly.

Utter paused, rubbing his jaw with the flat of his palm. He seemed honestly trying to remember. "Larsen said a funny thing, Stevens. 'We'll see you down in the Palo Duro country, Jack,' he told me before I pulled away. At the time I figured he meant I'd change my mind when they showed up—but now I don't know. Anyway, there it is."

The Palo Duro was a stretch of the Staked Plain through which the herd would pass in the next day or two. For what it was worth, Stevens concluded that Utter was passing on an honest warning.

"All right." Pat's wave closed the matter. "Just go on tending to your job, Utter. And after this let us know what you're up to. I don't give a hang," he proceeded frankly, "whether you get yourself killed or not. But we can't spare a hand for such foolishness."

Utter declined to express any thanks for his reprieve, but he looked relieved. Pat turned his back on him to call the rest of the camp together. From his urgent manner all guessed that a conference was in order. Noting Trinket Martin watching with interest from the wagon, he waved her forward also.

Waiting until he had the attention of all, he spoke bluntly. "I needn't remind any of you what we're up against here. It's another good ten days' drive to Matagorda, through danger all the way. These roans come first, and we won't have room for anybody who doesn't carry his own weight. Anyone got anything to say?"

The men looked at each other as if uncertain what to expect. But no one spoke.

"You're clear of Saw Log now," Pat told the girl soberly. "I'm not too sure of your safety with us all the way because, as I said, in a pinch the horses will have to be our first worry. Say the word," he offered, "and we'll leave you and Aunty at some snug ranch. There are two or three big outfits around here that you can absolutely trust—"

Polk Burnett had moved close to Trinket moments before. He waited anxiously for her response to this proposal. To his vast relief she did not wait for Stevens to finish.

"Would you—rather be relieved of the burden, Pat?" she queried plainly.

"No, no. It isn't that." Pat's face clouded. "I'm giving it to you fairly how matters stand. I just want it to be your decision, girl."

"Then we'll stay," she said with apparent relief. "I sold off my Saw Log beef before the drop. With luck I may be able to pick up a fresh herd somewhere along the coast." It was a cogent argument, the kind of thinking that led to a prosperous ranch. Pat's nod said that he fully approved. "Since Utter has warned us, surely we'll be safe with you as anywhere," she concluded.

"And with Stevens giving you another chance, Jumping Jack," Skurlock roared at Utter, only in jest, "you better shoot straight or I'll settle your hash myself!"

Utter looked briefly chagrined, covering his discomfiture with a sickly grin. "Keep on the jump yourself, Chunk, if you aim to beat me into that cavalry," was his muttered retort.

There could be little doubt that this practical reward, over and above their pay, was a far stronger deterrent to treachery than any form of pressure which might be brought to bear on these reckless rawhides.

"Okay. We know now where we stand," said Pat tersely. "Let's get the night guard posted and square things away here."

It had been decided to maintain a three-man watch at all times on the trail, and this was to be changed during the night. It amused Pat to note how young Polk extended himself to make sure the women were comfortable, in addition to seeing to his own duties. And tonight Skurlock, youngest of the owlhoots and likely to prove the most susceptible, vied with Burnett in his solicitous attentions to Trinket.

Burnett watched him with a scowl, and Stevens wondered how long it would be before this brand of competition made him boil over. Polk hung around jealously as long as Chunk made his show of helping the women. Aunty Thankful's barbed comments could not discourage the brassy owlhoot, and if Trinket was annoyed she was able to conceal the fact.

By accident half an hour later Stevens overheard Polk expostulating with the girl. "Blame it all, Trink! Don't be familiar with those birds. You don't know a thing about them—"

"That's true. I met you all together, didn't I?" she returned quietly.

"No, but I mean—" Badly confused by her implied coolness, he did not know what to say. "They're probably not at all what they seem. No telling what you might get yourself mixed up in!"

"Oh?" Her tone was dulcet smooth. "What should I know about them, Polk?"

"Well, there's—no telling." Burnett's growl showed that he was trying to convey the worst. "I don't trust a single one of them myself!"

Pat grinned in the dark. Probably Trinket was completely aware that the quartet were outlaws of the most irretrievable stamp. She must know also that Polk sought only to protect her.

"She can hold her own. Burnett will have to step fast to keep up with her," Pat mused, moving away as he became aware he was eavesdropping on secrets not properly his.

The night passed quietly, with the herd moved out on the open range to graze and bed down. The cries of coyotes came with a curious flatness on this level plain, and the late moon laid inky shadows under the brush.

Morning light was still shadowy and thin when a sudden violent disturbance erupted at the outer edge of the sleeping herd. The roans leapt up with a whistling blast of fear. Hoofs thudded as they started to churn in alarm. Sam Sloan and Alamo, on guard at that side, sought to check the gradually accelerating movement of the horses.

But the alarmed herd broke into a lumbering run, and the best they could do was to keep the animals roughly bunched. Laboring uninterruptedly, Sam raked the shadowy dawn-cloaked range with stabbing gaze, suspecting treachery of some kind. He heard Pat's authoritative orders, and in a matter of minutes the hands had the entire herd circling and milling. They halted it less than a mile from camp.

Hod Lewis and young Burnett were energetically hazing strays back out of the brush to rejoin the bunch, when Stevens came jogging around the edge of the herd in the strengthening light. It interested Pat to note that even Trinket Martin had piled out, racing along on her own trim paint pony to help stem the unexpected stampede.

"What set that off?" Pat sang out, glancing at Sam and Alamo for an answer.

The outlaw shrugged. "It was still pretty dark ten or fifteen minutes ago, Stevens. I never saw a thing."

"Me neither. Even if I did try," Sam said. "It was just one of those things, boy. Maybe a hydrophobia skunk spooked a couple of broncs. Or a gopher could've done it."

Pat asked a couple of questions, not unduly concerned. Any long trail drive was normally plagued with a thousand unlooked-for incidents of this kind. "No matter," he broke off briefly and named a fresh trio to take over the watch. "The rest of us will get back to the wagon and eat. It's time we were on our way again."

Old Kip, seldom disturbed by trail events, had

breakfast waiting when the crew arrived. Ezra and a couple of companions ate hurriedly and jogged out to release the guards, who raced in to gulp down a few mouthfuls while Kip snarled at them to hustle.

The first level flash of the sun saw the wagons trundling off across the endless plain. Its character was revealed in the morning light; Polk Burnett thought he had never seen such a perfectly flat expanse, without break or rise.

The sun rose bright and ardent, warming the faint freshness of dawn. In an hour it was hot. Later the sweat glistened on the smooth-flowing roan coats and the dusty riders mopping their red faces. Toward midday Pat indicated a change of direction to avoid the Palo Duro Canyon, an enormous gash, miles in length, splitting the flat plain. Although he and the Bar ES partners kept a strict lookout, no particular effort was made to circle the country they had been warned against. Nor did they see anything to cause alarm.

In early afternoon a couple of cowboys were spotted hazing a handful of steers along a mile away on the left, and later they saw a diminutive freight rig moving with antlike slowness on the horizon, its six teams kicking up a scroll of gauzy dust. There was no other sign of life except occasional leaping jack rabbits, and once a coyote swiftly faded into the dun brush.

That day saw them some thirty miles to the south of Tascosa. Burnett breathed easier, and the rough-mannered owlhoots jested and capered in a release of good spirits. The herd drew up fairly early, and Pat looked the roans over critically to judge their condition. Ezra conferred with him anxiously, and Sam had a solicitous comment or two to make.

Hod Lewis noted their concern. "What's wrong, Stevens?" he inquired gruffly.

"Nothing—yet." Pat spoke cursorily. "The feed up here on the llano is thin, and water could be a problem."

"Shucks, them salty broncs are in fine shape," Hod averred stoutly.

"Now, yes. Sam suggested we lay over tomorrow and make the last long haul down over the cap rock at night. But it's a matter of time. We'll shove off early," Pat decided, "and keep going to good water."

Lewis had the typical outlaw's scanty knowledge of stock handling, having long since acknowledged the superiority of Pat and the other Powder Valley men in this respect ."Anything you say," he conceded easily. "Every mile brings us closer to that cavalry, Stevens."

They thrust on in the morning, traveling steadily. The heat noticeably increased as they worked south. In late afternoon it became sweltering. A brown haze darkened the sky, presaging another storm, and Pat and the partners anxiously assessed their chances. Ez thought they were only a few miles from the south rim and advocated pressing hurriedly on. Recalling a narrow canyon three or four miles to the rear, however, Stevens ruled for turning back without delay. Rather than waste valuable time in indecision, this course was settled on and the herd promptly turned.

The first blast of sand-laden wind moaned across the bleak, shadow-darkened range as they headed the roans down a rocky defile into the lonely canyon. An unearthly light lay over the plain. During the next hour the blast rose to a wild shriek above their heads. The canyon filled with choking dust; the horses remained quiet, however, tucking their heads behind their shoulders.

Once more the crew skimped on food, and except for one hand who stood guard at the foot of the trail up the ravine, all sought what rest and protection was available during the stormy night. Before dawn the storm abruptly died away. Abroad early, Sam climbed out of the rock-walled crevass for a look at the weather and came whooping back down.

"Look alive there!" he bawled. "Fine day up on top, men. Time's awasting!"

Although breakfast proved a little gritty that morning, the weather, as Sloan averred, was clear and mild. Pat insisted on pushing on to good water without further delay. The herd traveled sturdily; well before noon they approached the break-off rim at the llano's southern edge, and a mile below a tiny creek came into sight. It was partially silted up with drifting sand, but offered a sufficiency of water for the herd. Here the roans drank their fill and rested an hour.

Thrusting on after a well-earned rest, the crew returned to its cheerful tone. "Ain't seen a thing of Blue Jaw Lasher," Jack Utter reminded everyone hopefully. "Shucks, he's forgot about us. From now on it's just work—and U.S. Cavalry, here we come!"

An hour later they were pushing straight south down a shallow canyon valley when Skurlock snuffed suspiciously at the steady breeze. "I smell dust, Stevens," he said. "Is that wind springing up again?"

Within minutes the faint scent thickened, a thin yellow pall rising far down the shallow canyon. Alarm awakened abruptly in Sam. "There's something going on down there, boys!"

Ezra set spurs to his bronc, intending to ride ahead and investigate. At that moment, a dark rumbling wall of moving bodies burst into sight at a turn in the canyon a quarter-mile below. Dust obscured all but the leaders, but Pat saw enough to comprehend. It was a full-scale cattle stampede hurtling toward them.

13

POLK BURNETT was one of the first to act. Ignoring the shouts of the men, he wheeled his bronc and raced back along the herd. Bringing up the rear in the Saw Log wagon, the women saw the puncher, racing toward them waving his arm urgently, without being able to see what it was that gave rise to his excitement.

"Turn back!" he yelled. "Turn the wagon and get going!"

Aunty Thankful, who was driving at the moment, heard the order. Instead of obeying at once she stood up. "Boy, what you yelling at us about?" she began. Able now to see across the brushtops, she abruptly understood. Her lean dusky face went gray. She hesitated no longer. "Hang onto that seat, honey," she rapped at Trinket.

The wagon nearly stood on two wheels as it came sharply about. She slapped the team with the reins, and the vehicle started back up the canyon, clattering and jumping.

Old Kip James, seeing his peril at almost the same moment, was little slower to respond. He cramped the camp wagon around, crashing through brush, and started off behind the others.

Having made sure of Trinket's safety, Burnett turned back. The hands meanwhile had not been idle. At Pat's shouted order, ignoring the thundering wave of steers bearing down on them, they crowded to the head of the drive and did their utmost to check and turn the roans.

It was far from easy. Panic struck the horses at

once; they churned and balked, striving blindly to break in any direction. The rumble of hoofs swelled, the cattle stampede threatening to inundate and trample Pat and his friends. Yet the outlaws stuck. Guns cracked, and their fierce cries rose through the uproar and the ominous dust that fogged the canyon. Pat cried warningly to the men, who had barely got the roans halted. In another minute the breaking wave of steers drove into the horses. For a brief space the confusion was indescribable. Equine blasts of fright and fury rent the air:

Barely saving himself more than once, Stevens saw the terrified roans gradually yielding to the terrific pressure. Not a one went down. Turning, the herd began to go with the stampede. There was an inextricable tangle of tossing horse heads and steer horns, and Pat found his mount moving along with the crush.

The impact of the two herds had slowed the stampeding cattle somewhat. Peering through the dust pall, Pat was encouraged when he glimpsed one after another of the crew, swamped and hemmed in, as he was, yet weathering the avalanche.

He set about working up to the front, keeping a tight control of his pony and all the while crowding the running animals and seeking to check their flight. The men took their cue from him. For a time it was impossible to tell whether it made any difference. Finally a perceptible slackening of the pace could be felt. Most of the roans were now in front, and it was possible to curb their speed.

"Hold them," Pat called across. "Snub them hard!"

Within a quarter-mile the frantic steers were slowed to a bellowing trot, and in another few minutes the running animals were brought to an uneasy halt. Fortunately, the turned wagons had been able to keep in the lead and were not overwhelmed. Pat took a hasty look about to check on the roans and the crew.

"Everybody all right?" he sang out to Sloan. "Where's Alamo—?"

"He's back yonder. Saw him just a while ago." Sam mopped his dust-smeared face. "Reckon we all came through it, boy. But it was close."

"Where's Ez?"

"He's checking on the roans. We're lucky, Stevens." Sam looked up shrewdly. "Crazy or not, I think that stampede was rigged on us."

Pat thought the same, but he wanted to be sure. "Diamond L." He read the brand on a brindled cow. "Don't know who that would be, way out here. . . . Did you spot any men at all with that beef?"

Sam shook his head. "Just that wall of horns coming at us, boy. Whoever set that off got out from under fast."

They were still tersely discussing it when Ezra hove in sight, jogging forward. "How did it go, Ez?" Pat queried.

Ezra looked sober. "Near as I know, okay. Didn't see a single bronc down, Stevens. With all our boys accounted for, that's damned lucky for somebody—"

In the midst of his talk a flat crack smote their ears, seeming to come from the shallow rim of the canyon. On the instant Sam's pony started to dance and paw the air. The stocky man fought it sternly, while Ez whipped his carbine out of the saddle-boot and threw an answering shot at random.

Dust fogged the canyon so thickly that few could see plainly for more than a dozen yards. The owlhoots left nothing to chance, sliding to the ground and dodging behind the cover of rocks or brush.

Sloan was more deliberate, and Pat made no immediate attempt to move at all. "Are you hit, Sam?" he barked.

Sloan waved a hand angrily. "That slug like to tore my spur off my foot," he threw back. "Even my bronc felt the jolt."

Further spiteful shots rang from the canyon rim, and the aroused owlhoots began firing in turn. "Get out of range, Sloan—you too, Stevens!" Skurlock rasped. "If that dust lifts they'll blast you out of the saddle!"

Satisfied that Sam was all right, Pat lost no time in taking this sensible advice. Ezra sought shelter near at hand. "Looks like Lasher's ambushed us, boy," he whipped out hardily. "If the stampede didn't work, he'll try to wipe us out!"

Pat was less certain of the answer. To him it hardly seemed the gunfire from the rim was heavy enough for a handful of determined renegades. It would take an hour for a couple of their hands to work up farther along the rim and close in from the rear, and Stevens was impatient with the necessity. On the other hand, any resolute attack while they were penned in the open canyon might pin them here for along time.

Before he could make up his mind one of the owlhoots gave a whoop of discovery. "Some old geezer riding this way from down-canyon right now, Stevens!" he sang out.

Pat took a cautious look. As Hod Lewis said, a mounted man was single-footing forward with singular indifference to his surroundings. He was old. The hands waited, taking in his ragged beard and battered, shapeless black hat. In the hot silence a last flat gunshot cracked from the rim.

The oldster jerked erect in the saddle. "Here! You, Kit!" he bawled. "Cut out that foolishness!"

There was no renewal of the firing as he rode forward. After a cautious delay a slim small figure showed itself alongside a high rock on the rim. "That you, Pop?" he piped in a breaking treble.

"It ain't nobody else! Get yourself down here, boy. Pronto!" The old-timer's order was vehement.

Stevens and the others cautiously showed themselves. Pat saw the outlaws exchanging sheepish glances across the brushtops. They were asking themselves if they had been put on the defensive by a single clean-lipped boy. "Is that what we all ducked and hid for—?" Pat caught Skurlock's jarring growl.

"Do I take it that's your son, neighbor?" Pat waved

toward the young lad sliding and clambering down the inside slope of the rim, barely ahead of his horse.

"That's him." The newcomer rode forward. "I'm Moze Lafey, stranger. My spread's over the rim four or five miles yonder——"

Pat nodded. "Diamond L, eh?" He introduced himself and the partners. "Seems like we unexpectedly ran into something here." He indicated the restless cattle.

Lafey grunted. "Mighty fortunate for me you did," he allowed gruffly. "Don't reckon I ever expected to see them steers again."

Pat made small talk for a minute or two while the lad approached, doggedly leading his shaggy-coated pony down the final slope. Old Lafey glowered at his offspring. "What was the idea of that gunplay, son?" he rasped sternly.

Kit looked surprise, peering blankly at the roan herd intermingled with the steers and then at Stevens and the other men. "Why, I——" he stammered. "Hang it all, Pop, I saw rustlers making off with our stock. They shot at me! There was three or four—I didn't dare show myself close. They started the stock up Comanche Canyon here, and I cut across the rim. I did what I could to scare them off——"

"Three or four, eh?" Ezra echoed with an edge to his voice.

"You didn't see 'em, Kit?" Moze Lafey put in swiftly.

"Not close——"

"How about you, Stevens?"

Pat shook his head. "No, there wasn't anybody with the beef. It was a roaring stampede when it hit us. They may have figured to pick it up later on," he added. He started to explain the drive to Matagorda, but Lafey had already gathered its import.

"That US brand you're driving is what told me you're on the level," he vouchsafed briefly. "Whatever happened, Stevens, we're plumb lucky you came along just when you did." He was looking at the roans anxiously "Hope there wasn't any serious damage to them fine broncs. I didn't see any critters down—"

"No, we got out of it whole. The most we lost was some time, Lafey."

There was discussion of how best to separate the stock without further delay. Moze said a wide stretch in the canyon valley a couple of miles below would afford room in which to work freely. Pat asked about the next water.

"You can water the roans at my ranch," Lafey offered.

"Nice of you," Sloan said. "And we'll help cut out your beef."

"Well, now." Old Moze swept them with shrewd eyes. "To be frank, it ain't often we run into honest men in this Godforsaken back country. We've talked about pulling out of here before this. Reckon you can figure out why."

Under Pat's direction the hands started drifting the mixed stock south. It was not long before they reached the wider stretch of the canyon mentioned by Lafey. A side canyon offered a convenient corral into which to shove the roans, where one man could hold them. A few hours' steady work saw the two herds separated.

It was plain that Lafey and his son would have trouble handling the still uneasy steers without aid. Pat directed Jack Utter and Hod Lewis to help drive the beef back onto its home range. "The rest of us will water the roans," Pat said. "And we may as well haul up here for the night."

"Not before we have a good look around though," put in Ezra bleakly. "Alamo, you and Sam cut a two- or three-mile circle around Diamond L and the canyon. You may pick up the sign of those rustlers—but let that go. Just make sure they're not hanging around here. If you spot anyone at all, let us know fast."

The men rode off to their various tasks. Stevens instructed Kip James to haul up the wagon near the Diamond L water and make camp. The horses were turned out on thin graze near at hand.

Twilight saw all in order. The men squatted on their heels about the wagon and voraciously stowed away a hearty meal. Alamo and Sam returned as the last light was dying out of the sky.

"What's the word?" Ezra asked crisply.

"All quiet," Sam said. "If them rustlers are still anywhere around this range they're well hid."

"If they figured to pick up the scattered stock, they'll be smart enough to guess something happened when it don't show up," Ezra opined.

Lafey and his son, who had been invited to eat at the wagon, listened alertly to this talk but made no comment. Conscious of this, none of the others mentioned Blue Jaw Lasher, and Moze was not asked whether he knew who the rustlers were. Skurlock and the rest of the owlhoots approved of this circumspection. It was the law of the range to be close-mouthed around strangers.

"I suppose you'll push on in the morning," Lafey remarked to Pat almost regretfully.

The younger man answered with a nod. "We aim to get these roans delivered and off our hands."

Moze could only agree with that. But they read his thought that with the Bar ES crew gone, Diamond L would once more be relatively unprotected. Stevens privately reflected, however, that the horse herd was only too likely to draw Lasher's renegades after it, if they did not give up altogether, and Lafey's spread would be safe enough.

Trinket Martin had ridden in to the Diamond L ranch house at sunset to visit with Mrs. Lafey. The house was the better part of a mile from the herd. It was young Burnett who noticed that Chunk Skurlock had disappeared immediately after supper, and he chafed with concern. Sam observed it.

"Shucks, boy! Skurlock won't be making any deals with Lasher at this late date, if that's bothering you," he scoffed.

"I'd be happier if I thought that was all," Polk said gloomily. "Trouble is, that big-chested Romeo is bothering Trinket again. I know what he's doing!"

Sam made no attempt to stifle a laugh. "Then what are you waiting for?" he jibed.

Burnett took the hint, getting up his pony in a hurry. Ezra watched him ride off into the dusk. "That young sprout ain't got his mind on his work, that's sure," he growled. But Ezra's bark was worse than his bite. He had helped promote more than one romance in his time, and he made no attempt to call Burnett back.

Polk was not far from the Diamond L lights when he discerned the shadowy shapes of two riders coming his way. "That you, Trink?" he called out.

"Right here, Polk," came her answer in an easy tone.

Skurlock was with her. He did not welcome Burnett's arrival. "Think I can't look after her without help, boy?" he sneered.

Polk's anger flared. "You weren't even asked," he retorted hotly, crowding his pony close alongside the other. "Why don't you go back to the brush, Skurlock, with the rest of the wolves?"

Chunk's answer was a sledge-hammer blow to the ribs, sweeping Polk out of the saddle and dumping him on the ground.

Trinket uttered a cry. "Polk, *don't!*" Dismounting hurriedly, she ran to him, thrusting aside the gun he was awkwardly trying to raise. "No shooting, do you hear me?"

"Get out of my way, girl," Polk said thickly. "I'll settle with that big brave hombre here and now!"

Skurlock sat his saddle squarely, laughing at them. "Don't fret yourself, Trink," he urged satirically. "He won't shoot nobody. He knows what'll happen to him if he does!"

He may have been right, but his scoffing tone was a strategic blunder. The girl stood erect between them, facing the nervy outlaw. "You can leave now, Skurlock," she whipped out coldly. "I find I won't need your help any longer."

Chunk's chuckle was uncertain. He was keenly

aware that for some reason he had got himself in wrong with her. "Don't tell me that punk kid rates a nursemaid because he stuck his neck out."

Polk rose to his feet, facing him in ominous silence, but it was Trinket who answered. "You may relieve yourself of any further concern for me," she said firmly and finally. "And I'll mention that my name is Miss Martin. I think you understand."

Evidently Skurlock did. Wheeling his bronc around with what sounded like a muffled oath, he pounded away. Trinket was solicitous as she helped Burnett to remount. Riding on with him, she showed a concern which suited the chagrined puncher to a T. So little did he understand women that he did not comprehend how this sudden switch in his fortunes had come about.

14

THE DRIVE SHOVED off in the morning, with young Kit Lafey waving good-by to Trinket. The roans appeared none the worse for yesterday's experience and made good time.

Low broken hills lay south of the Ilano rim for some miles. Working steadily out of these they found the land sloping almost imperceptibly downward toward lower ground. By late morning the sun was a blinding blaze in the coppery sky. But for a persistent, mild breeze blowing out of the south the heat would have been intolerable.

As the rangeland fell away they found themselves in a region of thick mesquite brush, head high. The time came when the brush stretched impenetrably on nearly all sides and they wove their way doggedly through the straggling openings. Faint tracks underfoot showed that this had been a seldom-used trail for many years.

Stevens happened to be riding in the lead when a clearly discernible fork in the trail appeared, marked by a sagging, bleached wooden sign. He and Ezra jogged forward to make out the faded lettering. RAT-TLESNAKE FLAT, 2MI. TAKE THE OTHER ROAD, the sign read. Canted drunkenly sidewise on its stake, it never-theless pointed definitely down the right-hand fork.

"We'll have to post a guard here to turn the broncs," remarked Ezra.

But Pat was not taking anything for granted. "Hold on," he commanded tersely. "We better haul the drive up right here for a look around." He knew the Brasada, a notorious snake country, lay somewhere in this gen-eral area. To make a mistake now might pose an even greater danger to the horses than the stampede.

Sam rode up while he was speaking. He looked at Pat oddly. "What do you mean, haul up, boy?" he argued. "That sign reads plain enough. We don't want any part of Rattlesnake Flat."

"That's dead right," agreed Pat. "Could be the sign reads all too plain. I'm asking myself if there's any chance it's been changed—"

The Bar ES partners looked at each other quickly. Pat's words put an altogether different face on the sit-uation. While no sign of Lasher or his treacherous con-federates had actually been seen, it would not do to assume they had given up and turned back.

Ez promptly wheeled, calling out orders for the herd to be halted. Hod Lewis and Alamo worked vigorously with the others to accomplish this and rode forward to learn what was afoot. Pat's doubts were explained to the pair briefly.

Lewis was quick to see the point. "I've been through here before," he allowed. "But I don't seem to recall this fork. . . . Come on, Ezra." He started forward. "We'll shove on down what it says is the safe trail for a look around."

Pat might have accompanied them, but at that moment Polk Burnett came riding forward. "Hey, Stevens!" he called, and Pat turned back to hear what he had to say. "The women want to know what the tie-up is. I expect they're afraid those Tascosa buzzards may still be on our trail."

Pat's grunt was noncommittal. "That's what we aim to find out, before we take it for granted they're not." He indicated the weathered sign at the fork and explained his doubts. "Hod Lewis and Ez are shoving ahead now to learn whether we can get through okay. They'll be back shortly," he told Polk.

Pat and Sam had barely turned for a brief scrutiny of the horse herd when a string of gunshots sounded flatly from the south. Polk alerted instantly. "Is it possible they ran into some of Lasher's men way down here?" he asked uneasily.

Pat declined to show concern. "We'll soon know," was his brief comment.

After a wait they heard pounding hoofs, and across the brush they caught glimpses of Ezra and Lewis driving toward them at speed. The pair burst out of the mouth of the supposedly safe fork of the trail, and the one-eyed tracker made an angry gesture.

"You were right, Stevens," he exclaimed, reining in. "Snakes all over in there! Hundreds of 'em!"

"Rattlesnake Flat, eh?" Pat was scarcely surprised.

"No name for it!" Hod Lewis burst out. "Stevens, there's a hole in the rocks down there that looks like a can of fishworms . . . all rattlers! Why, they're buzzing like bees, and it stinks to high heaven."

It was true that even this far away there could be detected a pervasive odor of musk. The roans were growing uneasy; they threw their heads up and snuffed the breeze.

Pat's nod was curt. "Not much doubt that sign was changed—deliberately. Alamo and I will try the other trail a ways to make sure."

Alamo was ready, starting off at the word. Pat was not far behind him. "Keep an eye peeled, Stevens.

Both forks could be loused up with the pesky rattlers," the outlaw warned.

They pushed ahead a mile without seeing anything worth noting. A like distance had nearly slipped by before Alamo suddenly whipped out his Colt, which banged instantly—and Pat saw a rattler writhing in its death throes at the edge of the brush.

Thus warned, they peered about with caution, but saw no further malignant signs of life. Five minutes later Stevens shot a rattler. Evidently the two were strays, not uncommon in this part of Texas. Hunt as they would they saw no further evidence of real danger. *"This* is the right trail," Pat concluded. "We'll head the roans this way and crowd through fast. I don't believe we'll have any trouble."

They turned back, smiling grimly when they saw the anxious faces of those who waited. "What luck, Stevens?" Jack Utter sang out.

"All clear." Pat announced. "We'll push on down the trail without any stalling around and you can tell Kip and the women to stay close behind," he directed Polk. "Skurlock, change that sign to point the other way before some unfortunate traveler runs afoul of it."

Chunk changed the sign, pounding it firmly into its original position with a rock, and he and Hod Lewis blocked the Rattlesnake Flat fork while the herd was turned into the other and urged along. Pat and the partners whooped vigorously until the roans struck into a brisk trot; and this time it suited Pat to see young Burnett hang back to accompany the Saw Log wagon.

Aunty Thankful had received the news of the rattlers with a tightening of her thin lips. Mortally fearful, for once she insisted that Trinket drive. Stevens grinned to himself at sight of the courageously determined woman sitting bolt upright on the wagon seat, her scattergun clutched in a death grip.

Tension did not relax as the brushy turns dropped behind one after another. The yellow dust boiled up under the pounding hoofs, the wagons bouncing along in a thick haze. At one point Aunty Thankful abruptly threw up the scattergun and blazed away. The team reared, jerking the rig ahead. Trinket had all she could do to master the frightened horses until Polk raced to their heads and forced them to behave. Hearing the shot, Stevens dropped back far enough for a quick look.

"All okay?" he called.

Burnett waved him on. "Aunty blasted a rattler to shoestrings," he threw back. "No harm done—"

"Nonsense! It was all her imagination," said Trinket severely. "I saw no rattler."

She was probably correct; but some inborn sense of fitness prompted Polk to defend the terrified woman. "Maybe not," he retorted. "But there's one laying back there blown in two—"

Gray as ashes, her eyes wide and staring, Aunty Thankful flashed him a look of gratitude.

It was the one scare they encountered. Half a dozen miles beyond, with the lowering sun threatening to drop below the horizon, they appeared to be far beyond the danger area. But Aunty insisted on pressing forward another mile or two, with a fearful backward glance.

The accidental circumstance of encountering a thinly grassed ridge with a tiny creek at its base decided the final halt for the night. Two hands rode about examining the range cursorily without locating any rattler sign. Pat saw that old Kip got his wagon set up in a convenient spot, and soon the odor of cooking food drifted from the fire.

Waiting to eat, Pat and the partners moved out a few rods apart for a word together.

"We're moving along good now," Ezra opined. "Getting closer to sea level all the time. Don't seem to me the air was quite as dry today."

Pat agreed. "We should get the Gulf breeze in another day or two." He paused. "I'm still thinking about that sign at the forks," he confessed. "We'll keep a close watch tonight just in case."

Sam grunted assent. "It could mean one of Lasher's wolves is ahead of us. Could they make trouble for us at Matagorda, boy?"

Pat didn't see how. "You never know. But I expect we've about got this drive licked. If we just watch our step from here on in," he added dryly.

A three-man watch was posted after supper. Sam joined the first trick. He heard a rattler buzz once during the night, but prudently vacated the vicinity. Nothing came of it, and the other hands reported all quiet.

On the following day, although it was sweltering hot, the air was fresher. Mesquite brush grew stunted, giving place during the afternoon to clumps of live oak and acres of open slough grass. Later they began to find rushes in the low spots. It was plain the coast was no great distance away now. The roans were living high on the lush graze and were easier to handle.

Next morning a couple of hours after the start Sam gave a triumphant whoop and pointed ahead. From a low rise Stevens caught the flashing glint of sunlight on blue tidewater. "Here we are. Tell the boys to haul up," he called to Ezra. "We better bat our next move around."

Ez stuck two fingers in his mouth, whistled piercingly, and waved the signal for a halt. He and Sam jogged forward to join Pat. "What now, boy?" the one-eyed man inquired.

"We better figure out how we're going to handle this," replied Pat. "There must be a coast road through here somewhere. I'm pretty sure Matagorda lies southwest. But we could get bogged down in these inlets; some of them cut pretty far back from the coast."

Alamo and Hod Lewis moved forward while they were talking it over. "What's the word now, Stevens?" asked Lewis gruffly.

"We're nearly there, Hod." Pat spoke quietly. "What about it? Do you boys still want in the cavalry?"

Lewis did not so much as hesitate. "Cripes, yes! We didn't come this far to give it up and turn tail."

He grinned. "I aim to see me in one of them yellow-striped uniforms, and maybe straddle one of these roans."

Pat nodded. "There's the little matter of finding the army camp next—"

"Why, there's a road of some kind yonder," Alamo cut in. "I seen a couple of Mex vaqueros driving a handful of longhorns along it, Stevens."

Pat looked up. "That so? Take a ride over there, Sam, you and Alamo. If you overhaul those punchers, ask for directions," he added.

The pair set off and within a half-mile struck the road. There was no sign of vaqueros or cattle, however. They pushed on a ways and Sam spotted a shacklike ranch house. An old man was pottering about the yard as they rode up. He scrutinized them out of slitted eyes, offering no word until they spoke up.

"Which way to Matagorda, dad?" Sam asked. He explained about the trail drive of army horses.

"Army post is yonder. . . . Camp Houston, it's called," the old-timer supplied briefly, indicating the direction with a gnarled finger.

Sloan gathered that he was not much for talking. "How far?" he pursued good-humoredly.

The aged Texan shrugged. "Till you get there," was his curt response.

"Okay. Thanks anyway." Winking at Alamo, Sam turned his pony. Not until they were well beyond hearing did either speak. "I know what's eating *him*," growled Alamo then.

"What's that?"

"The dang old fool takes us for outlaws!" Alamo snorted. "They've been hitting him for work and free meals, like as not. Anything for a recommend to get into that cavalry!"

"Oh well. Everybody makes mistakes." Sam's beady eyes twinkled. It did not escape him how these men had altered their whole cast of mind while working for a living. Having sloughed off his lawless proclivities with his occupation, Alamo was dead serious.

He could not wholly forget the facts of his situation, and he remained markedly sober as they rejoined the herd and Stevens gave the signal to thrust on. They turned into the sandy road and pushed on along the coast. Matagorda proved a matter of seven or eight miles, a low adobe and clapboard town lying back beside a broad Gulf inlet. On this flat land the saltwater sedge grew rank and tall. Pat suggested hauling up the herd on a low grassy swell a mile or so from town while he and Ezra rode on in to locate the military encampment and contact Major Couch. The officer had promised to be here waiting.

The roans were accordingly turned out to graze while the redoubtable pair thrust on toward Matagorda. Camp Houston, they soon learned, covered a considerable area at the upper edge of town. They rode down the main street of Matagorda, gazing about. Uniforms were common here, and it was plain that a large number of soldiers were barracked near-by. Ez called attention to the distinctive cavalry garb.

Accosting a redheaded sergeant, they were instructed how to reach Major Couch. They pushed on to the cantonment and made their way to Officers Row. A guard pointed out the major's cottage. Couch himself emerged on the boardwalk as they approached, he was in full regimentals, a sword slapping his leg.

"Howdy, Major." Ezra was casual. "Where do you want these roans?"

"Oh. Here, are you?" Couch's eyes glinted. "We'll just step down to the adjutant's office—"

He led the way. Entering a sweltering frame office building, the two were introduced with remarkable dryness to the officer of the day. Papers were drawn out and verified. Ezra averred the promised count was over if anything, but Couch would take nothing for granted. "We'll just check that detail," he said. "And we'll make sure they're the same horses while we're about it."

Ez glanced at Pat, his bushy brows twitching, as a cavalry corporal was called in and ordered out to the herd with a detail to check the count and the quality of the horses, and take delivery. "You'll help them drive the stock into our corrals, of course," the major snapped at Pat.

Stevens shrugged. "No harm done, I guess, after driving them this far." He and Ez led the detail out of town. The herd was in good order, the count rapidly made. Ez found time for a low-voiced word with Pat while it was being completed.

"These hard-boiled birds seem to take the quality of these roans for granted," he growled. "Mighty cool bunch, if you ask me!"

Pat had noted the same thing. "It's just another day's routine to them, Ez. No matter. Let's get this over, so you can finger your money."

The roans were driven the last mile and run into stout army corrals in ominous silence. Gesturing Pat and Ezra to follow him, the corporal led them to the quartermaster's office. Major Couch reappeared, and dogmatically saw to it that Ez was paid off to the last dollar. Ez signed the receipt and started to turn away, Pat at his side.

"Wait a minute there." Couch halted them with unnecessary curtness. "I'm directed to apprehend and hold every known criminal or outlaw who comes to Matagorda, for whatever reason. Sorry, Stevens—but I'll have to arrest you." Clamping his lips over the last clipped-off word, the major did not sound sorry, nor could there be more than a momentary doubt that he meant what he said.

15

PAT LAUGHED LIGHTLY and then sobered. "Not a very good joke, Major—after that long drive," he remarked.

"Unfortunately for you, it's no joke," responded Couch icily. "Let's not bandy words, Stevens. You're not only known to be consorting with outlaws, but I believe you're their acknowledged leader—"

Pat's brows hoisted. Before he could speak Ezra broke in jarringly. "Nonsense, mister! Are you crazy?" He gave the austere officer scant respect for his uniform. "I've known Stevens for twenty years and more. Why, dang it all, he's a respectable rancher and a neighbor of mine up in Powder Valley!"

Couch was not impressed. "Many a man has used just such a respectable cover for nefarious activities before this. Naturally, I'd expect you to stick up for your hands."

"Hand? *He* ain't no hand," Ez whipped out. "Say my son, and you'd come closer to it. Blast it, Couch, the boy was visiting us on the Bar ES the day you closed the deal for these roans—!"

The major had gone deadpan now, not even allowing himself a show of annoyance. "Let's not press the matter too far," he said. "It's true I found you and your disreputable partner on a ranch. I never bothered to inquire whether you were the legitimate owners, since the horses were my first concern."

"Fine pay you're doling out for all our work to make sure the cavalry gets those broncs," Ez fired out sarcastically. "Reckon I expected justice at least from the army. The more fool, I!"

"That's enough, Ezra." The officer froze up. "I'll

have to be the final authority here. Remarks will only get you in trouble."

"What do I care?" The one-eyed man's anger was ablaze now. "Throw me in the jug along with Stevens, if that's your style! . . . You've been listening to some troublemaker," he accused Couch. "An owlhoot himself, like as not. Show your guts now, and listen to my story for a change—"

Couch held up an arresting palm. Calling a guard from outside the door, he gave clipped instructions for Stevens to be placed in the guardhouse. "We've completed our business, and you can show this other gentleman the way out," he ended.

He seemed wholly sure of himself. Pat had sensed this moments ago and had abandoned any intention of attempting a serious protest. Ez would have argued further; but the major picked up a paper from his desk and appeared lost in his own concerns. Ez looked at Stevens blankly, and shrugged. Pat's answering smile was faint.

"Let it go, Ez," he said quietly as the guard started to lead him away.

"I won't." Ezra was grim. "I'll do something, boy. Don't know what, but—" He broke off in annoyance as an aide-de-camp sought to urge him to depart. Shaking his arm free, he stamped out of Couch's office muttering sourly to himself.

Ez lost no time in getting back to the camp outside of town. He was seen coming from a distance, and the owlhoots tensely waited for him to arrive. They were all near the camp wagon, listening alertly for his report, when Sam accosted him.

"How did it go, Ez?" Sloan had immediately noticed Pat's absence and was wondering what had happened.

"You won't believe me." Glum as he was, Ezra spoke up loud enough for all to hear. "I closed the deal for the broncs and got paid off—and Stevens was arrested as an outlaw and thrown into the guardhouse!"

For a brief space complete silence fell over his listeners. Sam's jaw dropped, then snapped shut with an angry click. *"Stevens? Got arrested—you say? What in the world led to that—?"*

If the outlaws remained soberly silent, Polk Burnett thought he had the answer. "Just as I expected," he exclaimed tightly. "One of Lasher's men got to the army first, Ezra! It couldn't be anything else!"

"Nonsense," Trinket Martin struck in tartly, jumping down from the wagon and marching forward, her eyes flashing. "That may be so, Sam—but there's no reason why the army should be more stupid than anyone else. Didn't you speak up for Pat, Ezra?" she asked severely.

Ezra's lean homely visage darkened. "Speak up for him?" he bellowed. "Why, I chewed out that stuffed-shirt major, girl—invited him to toss me in the clink along with Pat!"

"What did he say?" she pressed.

"Wouldn't even listen. He invited me outside, cool as you please." He repeated what he could recall of the exchange with Major Couch. There was little enough to give them the clue to the officer's incomprehensible action.

"Never mind. We get it," Skurlock said with gloomy conviction. "That about Stevens consorting with known outlaws is the tip-off. *We're* the outlaws, and Burnett is dead right—somebody got to this major's ear." He paused significantly. "There goes our chance to get into the cavalry!"

The others nodded, and Alamo and Hod Lewis glowered pointedly at Jack Utter. Clearly they thought his killing of Bat Hanlon at Tascosa to be responsible for this vindictive retribution by Lasher's gang.

"No—don't go off half-cocked about this," Ezra warned. "We don't know the answer to Pat's fix yet, and you came a long ways to get into that cavalry. Take it easy now. This could iron itself out yet."

"That may all be true." Clearly Trinket felt she had a right to take part in the sober discussion. "It still doesn't get Stevens out of the guardhouse. I'll get ready myself," she resolved on the spur of the moment. "I'll ride in to that army post and talk to Major Couch. He'll explain to me why Pat Stevens is being held without a shadow of proof, or I'll know why!"

"Don't do it, Trink," warned Polk, holding up a detaining hand. "Complain about Stevens now, and it could easily make his situation worse if anything. If army officers won't listen to Ezra," he sought to drive the point home, "will they listen to a girl—?"

This only aroused Trink's ire. "They'll listen to me," she declared. "Or they'll wish they had, when I turn Aunty Thankful loose on them!"

For a wonder, Aunty had thus far held her peace. But at this she put on a look of doom. She climbed down from the wagon as the girl turned that way, and swung into determined action.

"You gents will kindly look the other way for three minutes," she ordered brusquely. While they complied, Aunty helped Trinket struggle into a fresh shirtwaist and worked over her hair. Trink was ready in a remarkably short time.

By mutual consent the Bar ES partners joined the girl as she swung astride her paint pony. No one made any protest when Polk joined the party. It seemed logical that Pat's friends should want to do all they could for him.

Enviously, the owlhoots watched the four strike out for town. Trinket said nothing as she rode, her face set straight ahead. Thrusting on through Matagorda's busy main thoroughfare, Ezra led the way to the military base.

"That's Couch's office over there." He pointed it out.

Trinket made nothing of the armed sentry standing at the open door as the quartet drew up and dismounted. First on the ground, she ran up the three steps briskly. The guard automatically sought to bar her way inside until he learned her errand. There was a brief tussle as she thrust out her hands, brushing the rifle aside. The guard never knew exactly how it happened that she was past him so swiftly, striding into the major's office to confront the officer with flashing eyes.

"Sorry, sir. She—now—" the chagrined guard stuttered.

Couch's eyes took Trinket in fast. "At ease, soldier." He sat back, examining the girl with a pretense of severity. "To what am I indebted for this intrusion, ma'am—?" he began.

"That's what I am here to tell you . . . sir." Trinket made the salutation sting.

Flushing under his leathery hide, the officer slowly removed his cigar in belated politeness. "Guard! A—ah—a chair for the young lady."

"Never mind." Trinket gestured for the flustered young soldier to forget it, perfectly aware she was countermanding the order of his superior. "I can say what I have to say right here!"

But Couch was on his iciest good behavior now. "Is that—some of your friends outside? . . . Let them in, guard."

Sam and Ezra were champing at the bit by the time the rattled sentry thumbed them inside, and Polk was only a step behind.

"Now, ma'am?" The major was all business.

So was Trinket. "What's all this about your throwing Pat Stevens in the guardhouse?" she rapped out.

"Stevens was informed of the reason for his detention," replied Couch.

"So I hear." Trinket drew in a deep breath. "And is it your opinion I would have ridden here from Tascosa with an outlaw?" she demanded in a rush.

"My dear young lady—" The officer was clearly sparring for time now. She gave him none.

"Because the answer is, I wouldn't," she fired out flatly. "I insist on being told your reasons for believing I did. Mr. Stevens," she drove on, "is every bit as respectable as I understood you to be!"

Entertained by this forthright attack, once having got his breath, the major fastened his attention on Sam Sloan. "Mr. Sloan. You are Ezra's partner, I believe

—?" He paused. "Nothing was said in Powder Valley, naturally, about the crew you might pick up for the drive down here. But I've been given to understand—" he emphasized the phrase—"that you found it convenient to employ men specially fitted, shall I say, to aid you in passing through outlaw country."

Sam glowered at him. "Well, we undertook to make delivery—at your insistence," he retorted. "Regardless of insinuations, I didn't know my friends were liable to punishment for honest work performed. If I had it to do over, Major, you couldn't scare up enough money to buy our roans."

Ezra's disgusted expression backed up his partner's salty pronouncement. Couch scratched his head. "And do you insist, like Ezra, that this Stevens is an honest rancher?" he barked.

Ezra threw up a hand. "There you are, Sam. That's what we're up against! I'm a liar and Stevens is a crook." He whirled on Couch. "No, we don't insist on anything, mister. We don't have to. Are you telling us you never heard of the Lazy Mare there in Powder Valley?" he broke off incredulously.

"Oh yes." The major felt the barb. "Lazy Mare. The owner of that spread is probably in Congress."

Sam laughed at him. "He's in your guardhouse. Just don't come back to Powder Valley looking for recruits after this, Major—or horses either!"

Couch suddenly stabbed a finger at Polk. "*Is* Stevens an outlaw, or isn't he?"

"Why ask me? I'm just a hired hand." Recalling occasions when Pat had neglected to halt his hazing at the hands of the owlhoots, Burnett sounded deliberately evasive.

"Is he or not?" the officer thundered.

Polk shrugged. "He certainly knows his way around them," he allowed grudgingly.

"Polk!" cried Trinket in a scandalized voice, "You can tell the major at once what you know Pat Stevens to be!"

She was too late, however. Although there was more

talk, Couch appeared to have made up his mind with customary abruptness. He was noncommittal as to what his decision might be. "This will be taken under further advisement," was his final word, making it clear the interview was at an end.

For once even Trinket was at a loss. Waiting only until they were well away, she turned on Polk and gave him a tongue-lashing he would long remember. "Regardless of what you may personally think of Pat, this is rank treachery to your employers," she hurled at him. "If they pay you off now, it is well deserved!"

"Cut it out, Trink." Plead as he might, Burnett was completely dismayed. "The army must have something on Stevens. *I* don't know his history. . . . Shucks, I'll lie plenty for you, if that's how it is!"

Realizing his tentative jealousy, Trinket laughed at him without humor. "You're hopeless," she declared. "Go away."

His face woebegone, Polk unwillingly dropped back. But he continued to haunt their vicinity, which was easy since they had no thought of leaving Matagorda. There was further earnest discussion of how to aid Stevens. There seemed no sure means, but Sam would not rest satisfied until he had had his try.

An hour later Pat was aroused in his wooden cubicle not far from the guardhouse door by the sounds of a lively altercation. Someone outside was clamoring for admittance. A few seconds sufficed to inform him that it was Sloan, who was trying to bully, bribe or fight his way past the armed guards.

They dealt roughly with him. After a brief scuffle Sam's angry complaints ceased. Pat knew he was being led off the post. He shook his head. Here in the close-walled barracks under the blazing sun it was sweltering and all but suffocating. If even his friends could not reach him, there seemed little help to be expected short of a military hearing which might or might not acquit and release him.

Pat was still going over and over these thoughts when toward evening a fresh disturbance, briefer and far more puzzling, arose. A soldier arrived at the guardhouse whom Pat heard identifying himself as an orderly. "Corp'ral of the guard!" the cry rang out.

After a lengthy wait a fresh voice joined the rumbling talk outside. "Corporal of the guard reporting. What is it, Orderly?"

"Official orders for the release of the prisoner Stevens," was the terse answer. "You will comply at once, Corporal."

Pat's pulse leapt. What did it mean? His arrest had been a mysterious bolt from the blue, and his release was equally a mystery. But time enough to inquire further once he was out. He waited impatiently while the key-jingling guard stamped in and fumbled at the grill of his cell.

The gate swung back and Pat was in the act of stepping out when feet scuffed outside and a droning official voice crackled, "Delivering a prisoner. Guard is instructed to confine same to the guardhouse until further orders."

Prisoner and guard passed in as Stevens was making for the open and freedom. Pat swept the new prisoner with a searching look and abruptly halted in midstride.

"Hold on! Is that you, Skurlock? What in the world are you doing here—?"

Chunk avoided his eye and deliberately averted his face. Obviously there was something he preferred to conceal.

"All right, Stevens." Pressing close behind, the guard urged him on toward the door. "No conversation allowed with the prisoners. Move along, will you."

Pat, however, stubbornly tried again. "If someone is responsible for this, Skurlock, I want to know it," he insisted loudly.

Chunk shambled on without turning around. As he disappeared through the cell-block door, Stevens was tipped momentarily off balance by a vigorous thrust and a second later found himself out in the evening air. His cold insistence on receiving his six gun back only drew hard grins from the guard. "See the adjutant," he was advised.

"I will." Pat was unruffled. "In fact, I'll see Major Couch. Right now." He set off without waiting for more.

16

REACHING THE ONE-STOREY wooden office building in which he had last seen the major, Stevens started briskly up the short plank walk to the steps. The guard at the door stepped forward. If he was surprised to see Stevens free, his face was expressionless.

"Halt! No admittance, friend. Pass on." The flat order came by rote.

Pat stopped undecided, measuring the sentry with a look. "You're probably human down under that uniform. I have to see Major Couch, soldier—"

"Not here," the automatic reply rattled out. "The major's gone."

Pat turned away, speculating. With the abrupt setting of the sun the evening was rapidly turning gray.

Mess call rang on the air, with uniformed figures hurrying about the company streets. On the edge of the parade ground a two-man detail had only just lowered the colors.

This evening activity gave Pat an idea. Making for Officers Row, he reached the vicinity of Couch's cottage in time to spot the major striding toward it. The officer looked neither to right nor left, deep in thought until he heard Stevens call out urgently.

"Major—Major Couch."

He halted then, his keen glance sweeping around, and awaited Pat's unhurried approach.

"Major, why did you change your mind?" Pat challenged him directly.

"What convinces you I have?" Couch's marked dryness of tone said that he found it necessary to spar. "You're free, aren't you? Don't ride your luck too hard. Take a tip, Stevens, and be off."

Pat coolly declined to take notice of this advice. "I knew I wasn't guilty in the first place," he reminded Couch. "This whole deal smells like arbitrary authority, Major. I intend to know why my hand Skurlock was jailed—"

"Perhaps because we had the wrong man at first, and have the right one now," was the uncompromising retort.

"No, it won't do." Pat was firm. "You've been acting altogether too freely on loose evidence—or none at all. As a responsible officer, Major, I'm aware you must answer to a higher government authority. It'll save red tape if you tell me now."

Couch had had sorry acquaintance with bureaucratic detail in the past. His smoothly uniformed shoulders shrugged. "Oh well. If you haven't figured it out, Stevens, your—friend Skurlock came to me voluntarily and spilled the whole story."

Pat concealed his own faint alarm behind a show of incredulity. "What story—?"

"It hung together," the officer proceeded levelly, ignoring Pat's question. "You did face a problem in getting down across the Panhandle. And Skurlock knew I had word from up the trail, from a recognized outlaw named Lasher, that you were with the Bar ES herd and was one of his deserting lieutenants, hoping to enter the cavalry."

"*Me* enlist in the cavalry?" Pat's smile was grim. "Okay. Since *you* haven't figured out that Skurlock was lying to get me off the hook—"

But Couch calmly overrode him. "After Skurlock's story, I knew what kind of 'dealings' provoked your young puncher," he drove on evenly, "and why this man Lasher would use any means to best you. . . . He nearly succeeded, Stevens—but not quite. I'm not sure yet whether your actions could be considered entirely legal or not." The major's tone closed the door on further discussion. "Content yourself with that."

Pat urgently pressed for Skurlock's release, taking into consideration his honest endeavor in seeing that badly needed horses reached the army in time; but this plea received no encouragement. When Couch evinced impatience by brushing past him he gave up.

"I want my horse and my gun back, Major," he said abruptly. "Either I'm guilty, or you're using mighty high-handed tactics on me!"

All business, Couch called to a sentry, gave him brief instructions and turned away, striding briskly toward his delayed supper. The guard called out his immediate superior, relayed the orders, and Pat was led to a shadowy stable where his pony patiently waited. His six gun had been stuffed in a saddle-pocket. Saddling up, Stevens thanked the stolid stable-man and then rode away from the post.

Anxious to learn all he could, he passed up a meal in Matagorda and rode straight out to camp.

The cookfire was dying down, and he saw no moving figures about. "Anybody here?" he called, announcing his arrival from a distance.

After a delay a voice came out of the dark at one side. "Who is that—you, Stevens?" Sam Sloan was gruff with surprise. Further movement sounded at the words.

"Out, are you? This is good news, boy!" Ez was frankly pleased.

Pat heard an eager flutter as the women came forward. "Oh, Pat! How on earth did you work it?" breathed Trinket.

A final figure moved out reluctantly as if wondering what might be in store. Pat made out Polk Burnett's slim form and wary face.

"I know where Skurlock is. But where's the rest of the boys?" Pat asked.

"Old Kip's in town," supplied Sam. "Don't know where the rest went. . . . You know about Chunk, you say. What happened, boy? How did you get free?"

Pat tersely related how Skurlock had passed him at the guardhouse door. He repeated Major Couch's words, revealing that the owlhoot had spilled the whole complicated story of the actual events.

"I can't figure it out." Stevens was puzzled and bothered. "Chunk was helping me, of course. But he didn't have to do that. He'd already been paid off, hadn't he?"

Ezra nodded. "Paid 'em all, first thing. Anxious as they was about that cavalry, I didn't expect to see or hear of them again—"

"That's right," Sam cut in briskly. "We made delivery and got our money. With you in the clear, boy, what's there to prevent us from pulling out pronto and making tracks for home?"

Pat was cold to the idea. "No, Sam. I don't know how, but I'm taking Skurlock with me when I go—if he wants to go," he declared quietly.

Sam would have argued, scoffing that Chunk had been strictly on his own in what he had done. "It may even be his way of wangling an enlistment," he observed shrewdly. "After all, he saved that bull-headed major from pulling a real boner with you."

But Trinket spoke up pluckily. "Pat is right, Sam," she urged. "Whatever Skurlock's motive, Pat owes him the same loyalty. We simply haven't the right to leave one of our hands in the lurch like this."

Her calm identification of herself with their responsibilities earned a quick grin from Sloan. "I won't argue," he capitulated cheerfully. "Did that weathervane army feed you tonight before they tossed you out, Stevens?"

Pat admitted to not having eaten. Aunty Thankful took charge of the situation while young Burnett, who had not volunteered a word throughout, gloomily built up the fire. Later, while Pat stowed away food, squatting on his heels near the fire with the others standing near at hand, they soberly discussed what could possibly be done for the imprisoned owlhoot.

The prospect appeared hopeless. "It's a mighty serious offense to break a man out of an army guardhouse —even if that's possible," Ezra expressed the inner conviction of all. "As it is, I wouldn't be too sure that biggety major might not change his mind and grab us all."

Polk got up uneasily and walked a circle around the fire. Restless as he was, he failed to catch the jovial wink Sam tossed at the girl. After a tense delay the puncher whirled back toward the fire.

"Stevens, you'll admit every word I said to the major was strictly true," he burst out defensively.

Pat was mildly surprised at this uninvited attack. "That's right. Did somebody say different?" he countered.

But Polk was not to be turned off. "I won't have you thinking I was responsible for your landing in the guardhouse, or that Skurlock did my work in talking you back out of it again—!"

"I don't expect Major Couch took you as seriously as all that. Slack off, boy. It was Blue Jaw Lasher's scheme that tripped me up. Nothing you could say would have had the same effect as Skurlock's talk." Pat's tone was mild, aware as he was that Burnett was aiming his argument indirectly at Trinket.

Polk missed the irony of Pat's suggestion that his want of loyalty at a critical time was of small account. Although he subsided with an air of relief, the girl's look remained remote.

The fire was dying down an hour later when a gruff call from the dense gloom alerted them all. Sam and Ezra instinctively stepped back from the light, and Burnett moved toward Trinket as if he felt the need to protect her. Hoofbeats swelled and the approaching rider appeared faintly in the dim glow of the fire. "Where are you all?" he called out.

It proved to be Jack Utter, and they saw quickly

enough that he was alone. Ezra stepped forward. "That you, Utter? I don't see your pals—"

"Not liable to either. Alamo and Hod Lewis made it into the army. What do you think of that?"

"Hey, is that a fact?" Sam was deeply pleased by the announcement. He scratched his head, then resumed a critical tone. "How in time did they make it, anyhow?"

"Nothing to it." Utter was literally bubbling over with information. "They ran into an old buddy, Hype Taggart, who joined up a few months ago and made sergeant in a mule pack outfit. Hod and Alamo thought that was good enough for a start, and they got in on Taggart's recommend."

"But you didn't go in with them?" Pat was listening to all this with alert interest.

"No—I held out for the cavalry," Utter explained. "But I'll make it yet. We got it all figured out, and Hype is working on it for me."

Pat was hugely enjoying the ironic anomaly of these hard-boiled outlaws scheming and plotting to win to the hard and dangerous labors of army enlistment. It was another moment or two before he found an opening. "You heard about Skurlock, Utter?" he asked then.

"No, Chunk sort of disappeared on us, Stevens. We figured he was working some angle of his own. We did hear about you though," he went on. "How did you wangle your way out?"

"It was Chunk who talked me out of the guardhouse." Pat explained how Skurlock had foiled Lasher's scheming by going to Major Couch with the whole story. "I thought for a while it might be Chunk's way of getting in the service, but I don't know." He shook his head. "Is it possible that this friend of yours, Taggart or even Lewis or Alamo, now that they're in, could do something for Skurlock?"

Utter had taken the news with a frown, but he remained hopeful. "It's worth a try anyway. Hype knows Chunk, and I'll tell him about it." His look was dour.

"Kind of stupid of Skurlock to talk himself right into the jug, wasn't it?"

"I haven't figured it out yet," Pat admitted. "Skurlock doesn't owe me a thing. But I sure owe him plenty. I've made up my mind I won't leave with him still in the guardhouse. You know what it means to tangle with the army, Utter. It looks pretty hopeless, unless this Taggart can pull strings."

"Leave it to me, Stevens." Jack spoke with unexplained confidence. "I'll buzz Hype about it and see what can be done. They need mule drivers. Will you wait right here till I come back or send word?"

Pat said they would. "And thanks, Utter. I hope you make the cavalry all right. I can't honestly expect you to say or do anything that will endanger your chances."

Jack grinned. "I'm not doing any worrying. Don't you," he advised easily.

"It's not a case of worrying." Pat was sober. "Chunk stuck by me. It's my chore now to do what I can for him, and nobody else's.

Utter waved this aside. "I don't think he expects a thing, Stevens. He never meant no real harm to Miss Martin. We all liked her. Towards the last there, I expect Chunk figured he maybe owed *her* something." His eye strayed unbidden toward Polk Burnett.

Trinket pretended innocence. "That could hardly be the case," she said. "Anything I might have done for him I'd have done for any of you."

Seeing Burnett about to boil over, Pat struck in smoothly. "Well, no matter. I'll feel better knowing something's being done for Skurlock. Keep us posted, Utter. Will you do that?"

"Sure will." Jack was casual. He talked a few minutes longer, then showed signs of restlessness. "Better be on my way," he remarked. "I'm pulling a string or two on my own and I've got a man to meet in town."

As they listened to the fading sounds of his rapid departure, Sam shook his head. "Taken altogether, Stevens, those boys have been mighty decent."

Pat agreed heartily. "Just full of beans—that's what

lands most of their kind in trouble. Now and then a real bad egg like Lasher or Hook Larsen takes advantage of them—"

"You're too generous," Polk struck in with dogged irony. "There's not a one of that bunch that needs a nurse any longer." His brow knit in perplexity. "But what did he mean about Skurlock feeling he owed Trink anything?"

"He liked her, boy, and tried to show it." Ezra was dry. "It wasn't no more than you've been up to yourself."

Burnett felt the jolt, but still protested. "Hang it, Ezra, the man was a known outlaw! Does anyone pretend I don't have a better right than his?"

"Well, you might ask the young lady that." Ezra's drawl grew marked. "Still, you're right enough in one way. I don't believe Trinket was ever fooled for a minute. We were all on that drive together. She could've made a lot more trouble with that bunch than she did, if she hadn't shown good sense."

Trinket had retired to the wagon with Aunty Thankful at Utter's departure. She might well have been pleased with Polk's answer now, could she have heard it. "You're right." All the puncher's vehemence had dropped away. "It could have been a mess, Ez. I don't suppose I did anything to help matters much."

Pat clapped him on the shoulder. "Good man, Burnett. Keeep that attitude and I'll begin to think you're grown up. . . . Shall we hit the sack?" he broke off, speaking to the others. "Utter won't be back before morning anyway, and we may have a full day ahead of us."

The following day the hours dragged by, with no one visiting their camp beyond a stray Mexican or two. Kip James did not appear, and the women took over the task of cooking.

Pat remained imperturbable, but Burnett evinced increasing uneasiness. "What *are* we waiting for, Stevens?" he burst out finally. "We're all together, and we'll never have a better chance. Why not pull away from this country before we get further involved?"

Pat shook his head smilingly, and it was Trinket who answered. "He made his promise, Polk. Remember?" she chided.

Polk was secretly too relieved at receiving her attention to argue with her. "I'm only thinking of all that money Sam and Ezra are carrying," he returned lamely. "Blue Jaw Lasher must know it, and Hook Larsen too, by now."

The studious silence with which this was received seemed to say he was not the only one to have thought of it. Pat was himself growing mildly impatient for action. Toward sunset he was on the point of setting out for the army post to learn what he could, when they spotted a horseman riding their way in haste. Sam shaded his eyes.

"Well, what do you know!" he cried. "That's Skurlock himself—heading this way on the double!"

17

RIDING INTO CAMP, Chunk waved debonairly to all and was soon answering gruff queries put to him by Sloan.

Skurlock laughed indulgently, enjoying the stocky little man's incredulity over his replies, and faced Stevens as the latter came up. Pat met his look with one as steady. "Evidently you knew what you were doing when you turned yourself in to the army," he remarked briefly.

"You mean I must've had something up my sleeve?" Chunk looked surprised. "It's this way, Stevens. Utter cooked it up with the boys to spring me out of the guardhouse. The crazy fool even got himself arrested and thrown in with me to tip me off."

"He did?" Sam was agog with interest. "What did he do?"

"Raised a row in one of them army stables—insisted they shoe his bronc, or some such business. I heard he tripped over a guard and fell on him. One of Hype Taggart's friends grabbed Jack and ran him into the guardhouse to cool off."

"So they jimmied you out—?" Ez said.

Chunk shook his head. "No, I'm still under arrest —officially. I had to bribe the provost to let me out long enough to see you and Stevens. Hell, I don't want to be rescued!" he exclaimed explosively.

"You don't?" Pat was mildly mystified. "Why not, Skurlock?"

The outlaw gave him a shrewd glance. "No need for it. That crusty Major Couch as much as promised I could get into a freight battalion as soon as the army moves out. . . . I did him a small favor," he explained evasively.

Pat understood what the favor was. It concerned himself. But since Chunk obviously preferred not to talk about it, he passed it over.

"You're serious about this?" he asked Chunk. "Because you're still one of our boys, Skurlock. I stood ready to stick by you—here, or up north. There's even a spot for you on my spread in Powder Valley if you want it."

Skurlock looked partially stunned for just a second. Then he chuckled. "Afraid I wouldn't be interested in no bunch of cows with this break in the army ahead of me. Thanks, Stevens, but the answer has got to be no. If you see any of the boys," he pursued ingenuously, "just tell 'em old Chunk's okay."

"Sure will—but it's pretty unlikely, Chunk." For the first time Pat allowed himself a mild familiarity with the other. "You're the only reason we were staying around here. If it's a sure thing you don't need any further help, we're off in short order."

"Fine." Skurlock was unemotional. "No need to fuss about me for a minute. Fact is, I've got to get back to that guardhouse before I'm missed."

He stuck around a few minutes longer, visibly embarrassed. If Polk guessed that he wanted to speak to Trinket a last time, he showed no marked resentment. "I hope you have luck in the army, Skurlock, and—no trouble when you come out," the girl spoke up warmly.

"Thanks, Miss Martin." Chunk was briefly abashed. "Reckon you know I always wished you the best of luck, too."

He left shortly afterward, as casually as he had arrived. Sam began to laugh. "What an hombre! Bribed his way out of the guardhouse just to talk to us! Did you swallow that, Stevens?"

Pat shrugged. "You heard him. The fact is, all those birds were pretty much the same."

Ezra grunted acquiescence. "It's plain they savvy the army better than we do. I bet every last one of 'em will wind up in service, and make damn good soldiers too."

"They're men. Major Couch understands that much," Pat said. "And that's the kind he's looking for. In spite of all his loud talk it'll be forgotten what those four were if they toe the line. That kind is always a law unto themselves, but if they want to stay in bad enough they'll mind their manners."

"Yes," seconded Sam sagely. "Looks like we can stop bothering our heads about that bunch now."

"And start worrying about ourselves, you mean?" Pat nodded. "My idea exactly. I don't see any good reason why we shouldn't pick up our traps and shove a mile or two on our way right now."

Late though it was none of the others showed surprise. The money in their possession rested heavily on the Bar ES partners. Despite the nearness of Matagorda and the army post, it was by no means certain that an attempt might not be made to relieve them of it. The day Ezra was paid off Sam had seen to it that the camp wagon was stocked with such supplies as they would need on the way north.

Jack Utter had brought the information, which he thought funny, that even old Kip James was obsessed with the hope of getting into army service, and had procured a job as swamper in a saloon in town while he tried his luck, so Trinket asked, "Can I help by driving the camp rig?"

"Why not?" Pat saw that the answer pleased her. "You can swap tricks with Sam and Polk and give Aunty Thankful a rest."

The latter snorted. "Rest!" she muttered. "Since when did I need rest—or get any, for that matter? I'll be driving with that child's head on my lap, sound asleep!"

They set off presently, with the wagons leading the way. There was no difficulty about following the coast road north. In the thickening dusk they passed ranch wagons and freight outfits, all headed for Matagorda. Occasional riders looked the little outfit over with curiosity, but they were not accosted save by polite Mexicans.

Few as the landmarks were along the sedgy coast, Ezra knew when they reached the point at which they had struck the sandy road. "We might as well back-track, boy," he remarked to Pat.

Stevens only nodded. The thin sickle of the moon revealed a grassy sea, which seemed endless. Once away from the road they saw no sign of life beyond the marsh birds they disturbed on their nests.

They pressed on for an hour across steadily lifting ground until open range land surrounded them on all sides. The wagons were hauled up on a little flat beside a low creek, and the horses were turned out.

"We keeping a watch?" Sam queried.

Pat's nod was not delayed. "One man will do," he ruled. "If you can stick it out a couple of hours till midnight, Sam, wake me up and I'll take over."

No fire was needed, and within a remarkably short

time the camp was dark and silent. It was rather later than midnight when Sloan nudged Pat in his blankets, and the other rose to relieve him. "All quiet?" he asked.

"Nary sound," replied Sam. "Except the broncs stamping and tearing grass. I kind of miss a coyote howl or two down here." He chuckled.

"A few years ago you'd have heard them—only it would have been Indians." Pat stamped into his boots and moved off for a look around.

Ezra was first up in the red-streaked light of early dawn. He barely had a fire going before Aunty Thankful hobbled down from the Saw Log wagon with early morning stiffness and briskly took charge. "I declare if I don't take rheumatiz in this damp air," she grumbled.

For all her complaints the energetic woman had breakfast ready in short order. All were cheerful this morning with the possible exception of young Polk, who seemed habitually glum and whose glance was constantly drifting in Trinket's direction.

Pat noticed it, and noting also that the girl seemed utterly unaware of the puncher's attention, he could not help asking himself how the situation would turn out. It was true that girls were naturally adept at giving their admirers a difficult time of it, and Stevens had not yet been able to make up his mind whether Burnett would prove to be Trinket Martin's destiny or not.

The little train was on its way early. By midday they were back in brush country once more, and during the afternoon a low, yellow pall of drifting dust could be seen above the low swells. Later they caught glimpses of a cattle drive several miles away. It did not move their way, and still later the yellow smudge died out to the south. But the incident apparently set Polk to thinking. He stared stonily in Pat's direction two or three times and finally crowded his mount forward.

"You were in an awful sweat to head north again,

Stevens," he burst out, "worrying so much about those tough owlhoots that you plumb forgot about the rest of your friends!"

"I take it you're not speaking for yourself, Burnett, since you're still being paid." Pat looked as surprised as he was annoyed by the puncher's outburst, yet his tone remained mild. "What brought that on?" he inquired.

"Forgot, have you?" Polk sounded strongly incensed. "I'll just remind you that Trinket wanted to buy beef down here along the coast to replace her herd. And you hustled her off so quick she never had a chance to look around for any!"

The puncher mistook Pat's absent look for chagrin. "What about it?" he barked. "So long as those scrubby outlaws got what they wanted, doesn't it matter whether she does or not?"

About to reply sharply, Pat paused to run a big palm across his mouth. It occurred to him that Polk's charge was simply another ruse to gain the girl's sympathy.

"Never mind," Stevens gave back in a bored tone. "If I know what I'm doing, I expect you can wait and find out."

"Now that's gospel truth," struck in Aunty Thankful from the seat of the lumbering Saw Log wagon. "Are you boss here, boy—or do you just work for folks like I do?"

Trinket was taking it all in as well, her clear young features cool and remote. "Pat has promised me nothing that I can recall," she observed pointedly. "It was you who proposed we accompany the drive for safety's sake, Polk. I did think of buying cattle; but around Matagorda the small ranchers are holding out for an impossible price in the hope of selling to the army. I made it my business to learn that much."

Burnett's crestfallen face revealed how foolish he felt before this double defense of Pat's course. "Well, I still think it's pretty shabby," he muttered reining back as if only too acutely aware that he was unwelcome just now.

"Wait, boy," was all Pat said. "You'll see."

Starting out on the back trail it had seemed at first that the absence of the unpredictable owlhoots might well lighten the mood of them all. But Polk's manifest unhappiness laid a pall over the journey. Aunty Thankful tossed her head over the unreasonableness of young folks; but if she had any real preference concerning the outcome she concealed it, her manner impartial toward both Polk and the girl. Trinket alone appeared wholly oblivious of the puncher's anxious siege, and Stevens concluded this was by design.

On the following day they struck the vicinity of Rattlesnake Flat. This time there was little need of precaution beyond putting an outrider in the lead. They had luck driving across the dense brush. Ezra and Pat fired at a couple of rattlers stretched across the trail, but Aunty Thankful found no opportunity to discharge her scattergun—she showed no signs of relief, however, until the area lay well behind them.

Next morning Ezra began to watch alertly to the fore. "Ought to strike Lafey's Diamond L before long," he announced. Polk put the proposition that they might conveniently circle Lafey's ranch and pass on upcountry, but Pat said no.

An hour later they recognized the landmarks around Lafey's Diamond L. There was a flat-topped butte they had seen before, and the hills looked familiar. Not long afterward, passing over a rise they glimpsed a small bunch of Lafey's Diamond L stock.

Pat pointed it out to Trinket. "There's your beef, Trink," he announced. "But don't say anything when we meet old Moze. Let me handle this."

Burnett heard him and put on a look of disgust. "So you had this up your sleeve all the time, Stevens? What makes you so sure Lafey will sell?"

Pat shrugged. "I said leave it alone, didn't I, till I see what I can do?"

Polk would have retorted, but at that moment a bee

buzzed between them. Ezra sang out even before the faint crack of a gun reached their ears. "Watch it, folks! Somebody's shooting at us!" He pointed out a falling twig snipped from the brush near at hand. The wagons hurried on to haul up in a convenient hollow and the riders scattered.

"Who can that be—throwing lead before we make a move?" Sam called to Stevens.

"Either old Moze or the boy. Who else?" Pat was terse. Bidding the others wait, he rode up a slope and showed himself on top of the rise, waving his hat. *"Lafey!"* his rolling call ran down across the grassy swells. He was taking a chance, but no further gunfire sounded and shortly afterward a faint hail could be caught. They waited. It was ten minutes before old Moze Lafey pounded up on a salty bronc.

"That you again, Stevens?" He was all apologies. "Hang it all, I was hoping you'd come back this way, but I didn't dare expect it. All hell tore loose after you left here and I'm about ready to call it quits!"

"That so?" Pat was only too ready to draw him out.

Moze jerked a grim nod. "Rustlers have been hounding me to death, Stevens, and I may've lost a few head. Only saved what I did by riding night and day."

He looked haggard and worn out. "Kit was fired on two days ago. He got a nick on the leg and I'm plumb scared to let him ride line." He shook his grizzled head. "Don't know how much of this stuff I'd get to market if I tried to drive it!"

"It puts you in a pickle and no mistake," Pat conceded. "Why not sell it, Lafey?" he said reasonably.

The rancher's jaw dropped. "Who to—way out here? Don't make me laugh, Stevens!"

Pat's answer was deliberate. "I'm a cattleman. I might take the stock off your hands, Lafey, range delivery right here—if that fact was reflected in the price," he added cautiously.

Lafey immediately assumed a blank air. "We can talk it over anyway," he allowed. "Come on into the ranch, you folks, and rest your saddles." Turning, he led the way.

They did talk it over, continuing on through supper, with the result that before they turned in Pat had made a very reasonable bargain for the Diamond L cattle, while the Lafeys expressed relief at the prospect of abandoning this remote and unprotected range for good. Old Moze thought he might return to East Texas, where range land was priced higher but where he had done well. Certainly he did not regret selling his herd at a modest sacrifice.

18

"Do you think Mr. Lafey would honor my check for his stock?" Trinket asked Pat the following morning after breakfast. "He says with his herd sold he'll be pulling out. He might have trouble cashing it where I'm unknown."

"No need," Pat assured her promptly. "Sam and Ezra can lend you the cash. We'll be right with the drive, and you can pay them off when you get home."

"It would help." There was no false effusiveness in the girl's gratitude. "They'll have every right to collect interest on their money, and I'll be glad to pay it."

Pat smiled. "Don't suggest it until they do," he advised. "I know that pair. They may figure they have the right to do you a small favor."

She looked at him wisely. "You have all been wonderful to me from the start. From now on I intend to work too."

This was the day the roundup of Diamond L stock got under way, and Trinket was as good as her word. The men soon found her as adept at handling cattle as themselves.

This was wild range land, with no near-by ranches. The steers took to the brush country like deer, and old Moze thought there were moss-horns under the Diamond L brand which had not been seen for months.

The first hundred or so steers were easy to gather. On the second day, however, it was harder to locate the lurking strays; and once found, it was infinitely harder to drive them. Ezra and Sam soon hit on the expedient of working as a team, and this promised better results. But by the end of that day Lafey was by no means satisfied that they had rounded up all of his scattered beef.

"Must be dozens of them critters hiding out in the rough," he averred doggedly. "And your offer included helping to run 'em down, Stevens. Why leave a lot of good beef for the wolves?"

Constantly working farther away from the ranch, the riders found themselves in rugged country. A close watch was kept, since Lafey and his son had had so much trouble with rustlers. Nothing happened until the third morning, when the Bar ES partners, working together in the cut-bank breaks over west, suddenly spied a pair of cattle thieves in the act of driving several young steers directly away from the ranch.

The renegades spotted the grizzled pair at almost the same time. One of them threw up a carbine and fired. The slug whined overhead and was promptly answered by Sam, who despite his awkward obesity displayed considerable agility in handling firearms.

The partners separated and determinedly began to close in. For a matter of minutes the cattle were hotly disputed. The necessity to cling to the open while driving the animals shortly discouraged the rustlers.

As if at a signal they broke suddenly and fled, racing away through the brush.

"Is that some of Lasher's crowd?" Sloan whipped out.

Ezra hesitated. "Couldn't recognize them," he owned finally. "They're probably a couple of small-time operators. If we can nail them we'll soon find out."

"Let's go about it then," said Sam.

The pair set off in a pursuit that came close to being their undoing. Tearing after the fugitives at a break-neck pace, they found themselves plunging down a winding wash, and at a particularly sharp turn they were met by a crash of gunfire. It was plain the rustlers had planned to lay an ambush. Only the explosion of terror displayed by Sam's pony saved him from being shot out of the saddle.

The bronc reared and bucked wildly, giving its rider a thorough shaking-up. Ez had instinctively reined aside against the wall of the wash, and this had put him outside the narrow aim of the renegades. He unlimbered his Colt in a twinkling, firing toward the spot where his single sharp eye detected drifting gunsmoke. The fire from the rustlers ceased momentarily.

Sam was no more than seconds in mastering his mount. "Get over here!" Ez yelled at him. Even as Sloan reined over to join him they caught the scrape of hoofs from farther down the wash.

Though they pounded hard in pursuit, the quarry raced on in the lead. Presently even their tracks disappeared. Several minutes were lost in ascertaining where they had climbed out of the wash. Reaching level ground once more, the partners gazed over an unbroken area of heavy brush, with no evidence of the fugitives in any direction. Ezra reined to a halt.

"No use." He was brusque. "We could chase these birds clean to New Mexico and not catch up in this mesquite."

Sam was incensed over the escape of the rustlers, yet he sensibly agreed. "We saved the cows anyway.

Thing is to gather 'em up and drive on out of this God-forsaken country."

They turned back, gathering in the yearlings on the way. Since neither was injured there seemed no point in alarming the women with a report of their adventure. Taking him aside, Ezra informed Pat briefly about what had occurred and the matter was allowed to drop.

By evening another score or so of strays had been combed out of hiding. Stevens expressed the opinion that it would not be worth the labor to hunt for the few remaining head scattered over square miles of impenetrable brush. Lafey was satisfied. "We scraped up another thirty head or so more than I thought I owned," he vouchsafed.

Trinket had been instrumental in swelling the total, and since it was to be her herd, no one had worked harder or more diligently than Polk. "Now to get these babies north to the Saw Log range where they belong," he remarked, scrutinizing the two hundred and fifty head that had been thrown together.

Pat hid a grin at his proprietary air. If the girl also noticed it, she did not make overt response by so much as glancing in his direction.

It was an almost gala supper that Moze Lafey's wife served that night in the weathered Diamond L ranch house. Sam, Ezra and Lafey were absent on watch, and as soon as Pat, Burnett and young Kit Lafey had eaten they swung astride and rode out to relieve them.

The trio rode in and ate heartily. Sam then called Trinket aside and the financial details of the transaction were completed. Between them, the partners produced the payment for the steers without straining their resources noticeably. The girl gave them a note of hand to cover the amount until she could reach her own money at home.

A close watch was maintained throughout the night, as much because the stock showed a strong inclination to drift as to protect it against possible foray. Happy to be relieved of a troublesome responsibility, Lafey was on hand with the first streaks of daylight the following morning.

"Reckon you'll want to slap Miss Martin's Saw Log brand on them cows right off," he hazarded.

Recalling his own and Ezra's experience, Sam promptly demurred. "It'll take too much time, Lafey," he said. "We all want to get along home."

"That's true," Trinket seconded him. "And I intend to help with the drive."

Lafey seized on this at once. "You'll need all the hands you can get," he averred. "So what about that camp wagon of yours, Stevens? I can use a good stout rig to move my family east—and you won't have to spare a driver."

After brief thought, Pat was agreeable. "It's time Sam and Ez bought a new ranch wagon anyway—and they won't do it till they're forced to. We can load a couple of pack horses and throw the rest in Trink's wagon."

This arrangement was accordingly effected. The vehicle was turned over to Lafey for an extremely reasonable price, packs were lashed on a couple of broncs, and at an early hour the new Saw Log herd was headed north.

It proved an arduous day, with the cattle attempting repeatedly to break back to familiar home range. Trinket did her part valiantly despite the adjurations of Aunty Thankful, and Polk was furiously industrious. It was as though he not only took keen pleasure in working for her, but was bent on establishing his personal interest in the stock at the outset. Sam twitted the puncher over his unwonted industry, but Trinket wisely pretended to be unaware of it.

She appeared in fact calmly resolved to hold Polk severely at arm's length. For his part he was so thoroughly subdued by her disfavor that he wore a cowed look in her presence and even forbore to argue with the others. Watching Polk covertly, Pat could see that the girl had become so important in his life that winning her favor back was the only thing that held any real meaning for him.

They made a good dozen miles that day, and when they hauled up to bed down for the night, it was possible to make out the southern rim of the Staked Plain, bounding the horizon another half dozen miles to the fore. They had long since left the humid airs of the coast behind. Once more the air was dry and astringent.

"We'll top out on the cap rock tomorrow," announced Ezra at supper. "After that the infernal brush won't be so thick and bothersome."

The next day was also a strenuous one. The trail up to the rim was tortuous and winding, and the stock had to be kept closely bunched to avoid scattering. More than once a head or two escaped into a side wash, from which the task of extricating them was far from easy. The steady climb likewise slowed the rate of travel. The stock had to be urged forward constantly.

By early afternoon they won up to the level of the llano and all relaxed somewhat; before them the brush-strewn prairie stretched in an endless sea. The steers had been watered in the canyon during the late morning, but with heat reflecting in an ovenlike blast from the baked soil, they were soon in torment. Once more the problem of visibility arose as plodding hoofs kicked up dust, which rode with them this time on the ceaseless wind from the south.

Pat solved this problem to an extent by driving north on a zigzag course, so that much of the burdensome dust whipped away. But the task of driving hour after hour was onerous at best. By midafternoon they looked down upon a shallow canyon gashing the great level expanse. Investigating, Ezra announced that water and grass were to be had on its floor. It took the better part of an hour to find and negotiate a practicable trail to the bottom. Here it was determined to spend the night, since the natural boundaries of the canyon would eliminate the need for posting a guard.

All hands took a well-earned rest while waiting for supper, and it was only Polk Burnett who rode restlessly about examining the canyon's bed in the remaining daylight. He returned to camp barely in time to share the evening meal with the others.

"Thinking of homesteading down in here, boy?" Sam twitted him. "You sure did your exploring beforehand."

It was a fact that the remote and lonely canyon might comfortably accommodate a modest-size ranch. But Polk only shook his head curtly. "Looking out for tracks, Sam," was all he said.

"Find any?" barked Ez curiously.

Polk shook his head. "No."

Except for the occasional yelps and wails of coyotes, the night was uneventful. Pat aroused the crew early to take advantage of the morning air.

On this day many long searching looks were cast ahead over the level, seemingly boundless plain. While it had not been discussed, no one had forgotten Burnett's grim hunt for tracks the previous evening.

The sun proved so broiling hot that day that the herd was halted for an hour at noon, the steers allowed to seek what meager shelter they could find beneath the scanty brush. A few browsed on mesquite beans, but most were too thirst-ridden to take any interest in eating.

Pat and Trinket sat for a while in the shade of the Saw Log wagon, while Ez and Sam leisurely rode around the resting herd. Polk stayed away as long as his desire to be near the girl would let him. He moved forward finally to accost Stevens.

"I don't know if you've thought of this," he opened up abruptly. "But if Lasher's crowd is still hanging around Tascosa, Stevens, this beef will be bait for them. Blue Jaw hates you enough to make a fight for it."

Trinket's eyes opened wide at this reminder of danger ahead. "That's something I never thought of! But Polk is right," she said with unexpected decision, looking at Pat.

The latter nodded. "It's been in my mind," he allowed. "We'll talk it over with the boys, since they've got a stake in this herd."

No opportunity offered before that night, when they hauled up on the flats to bed down. Once the cattle were settled a single man was sufficient for night guard, and Burnett took the first trick.

While the partners were eating Pat broached the question of the hazard Tascosa might present. The pair made no pretense of hiding their concern. "It's a dozen to one Lasher is back there," Sam opined, "if he ever left town at all. He'll be wrathy because we beat his little game with those army horses, too."

Ezra was equally of the opinion that Lasher would do anything in his power to sabotage them. The subject was discussed at length. It was Trinket who finally outlined the most reasonable course.

"If we once get the stock on Saw Log range, the outlaws may never think of moving against it—except as they need a side of beef," she said. "I don't pretend to advise you men. But my own idea would be to detour Tascosa widely enough to avoid calling attention to ourselves."

Pat nodded agreement. "I think you're right, Trink," he observed. "It's just common sense, and it can't do any harm to try it that way."

It was all right with Ez and Sam. They were still a good two days' drive south of the Canadian. It would be time enough tomorrow to swing out of the straight course for a long detour. The decision lightened their spirits. Not even Polk demurred, since it would be folly not to avoid possible trouble this close to Trinket's home range.

Thrusting on the next day, they turned east in mid-morning and soon found themselves in broken, rolling country. This far north the slow erosion of creeks and canyons had carved the level plain into rugged, low hills. They maintained a constant vigilance but avoided observation from afar by staying well between the rolling swells.

During the afternoon Ezra appeared about to speak to Pat, only to desist. Later Stevens saw him conferring briefly with Sam; and it was Sam who finally accosted him, speaking in a puzzled tone. "Are we crazy, boy?" he asked. "I won't swear we saw anything; but Ez and I both got a hunch we're being watched—"

Pat's quiet nod settled his doubts. "We are, Sam. I noticed it an hour ago. I thought I was imagining things. But when I saw a dodging rider the second time, I knew." He was silent, his gaze roaming the distant brush. "They've spotted us," he said then with finality.

Ezra came single-footing forward as Pat spoke. The lanky redhead barked, "What about this, boy? Shall we knock off one of these gents to teach them manners?"

Pat did not take the query seriously. "One thing is sure," he averred quietly. "If they catch on that we're circling Tascosa to avoid them, it'll be a sure tip-off for Lasher. He'll come piling down on us like a ton of bricks."

"What then?" Sam demanded.

Pat shrugged. "It's Trink's stock," he pointed out. "She ought to have the final say. But if it was me I'd swing back to the trail and plow straight through Tascosa under Lasher's nose."

Sam hailed Trinket, waving the girl this way. The knotty situation was explained to her and Stevens repeated his cool proposal. She did not take long to decide.

"Sam and Ezra should have a vote in this matter, with their money at stake. But you were right before about the horses, Pat," she said. "It does seem that a stern, unyielding course has the best effect with Lasher. Do as you think best," she ruled simply.

"I had you figured to see it that way," Pat said. "I needn't say there's no telling what may come of this, Trink. But we'll do our damnedest."

Separating, they set to work at once, and a short time later the herd struck off in a fresh direction—straight for Tascosa and whatever trial awaited them.

19

Young polk was deeply worried as time passed and Tascosa loomed closer. Even the complete absence of any opposition to their steady progress seemed ominous to him.

It was Trinket for whom Burnett was chiefly concerned. "Nearly your last dollar must be tied up in this beef, Trink," he told the girl earnestly. "It would be hard lines to have to pay for a dead horse after the steers have been stolen—"

Strangely enough, she apparently failed to notice his mixed metaphor and his unwonted familiarity alike. "I'm quite sure Pat knows what he is about," she returned mildly. "He hasn't made a serious blunder yet. And it's true that only boldness will succeed with the outlaws. They know no other law in their own lives."

Polk thought this might work up to a certain point, and then backfire disastrously. Trinket sought to reason with him, her tone unusually temperate. Riding farther down along the drive, Pat noted the length and absorption of their discussion. After a time he jogged forward without haste. Polk took prompt advantage of the opportunity thus offered.

"You could be right not to give Blue Jaw Lasher an inch, Stevens," he said. "But we don't have Skurlock and those other tough owlhoots with us now to help back us up."

"That's right, we don't." Pat did not appear overly concerned.

"And another thing," Polk rushed on. "These steers aren't wearing the US brand either! That won't hold Lasher off this time." He drove the point home almost triumphantly, seeking to persuade Pat of how bitterly slim their chances were.

"That's just where you're wrong." The older man caught him up coolly. "It wasn't till I recalled we didn't take time to overbrand these cows with Trinket's Saw Log iron that I knew how right I was. Just leave this to me, boy," he advised firmly, flashing a tight grin.

His assurance was mystifying even to the girl. It drew her and Polk together in a common bewilderment, as Pat might have guessed it would. They watched him rack forward to the point as the trail dipped down toward the still distant banks of the Canadian and the cottonwoods lining the river bottom came into view.

"He must have some harebrained plan," Burnett muttered dubiously. "If Lasher's crowd is still in town —and they're pretty near bound to be—it better be good."

Despite her confidence in Stevens, Trinket drew comfort from the puncher's sincere concern for her welfare. Glancing about, she saw Sam and Ezra working industriously to keep the herd moving smoothly forward. "We must do our part, Polk," she murmured, urging her pony into action.

The steers had long since smelled water ahead. For some time all were busy helping to keep the brutes in a semblance of order. It was not easy going along the narrow winding trail leading down to the river crossing. The thirsty steers showed a tendency to spread out across a wide front along the shallow Canadian. Pat and Ezra kept them straightened out and moving on across before they drank too much and foundered.

Clambering up the low bank on the far side with water streaming from their hocks, the steers funneled into the end of Tascosa's Main Street, their uneasy bellowing and the low thunder of their hoofs echoing loudly. For a time the crossing kept the drovers too busy to think of anything else. The cattle rumbled into town, horns tossing at these totally unaccustomed surroundings.

The racket quickly warned Tascosa's inhabitants that something unusual was afoot. Booted and belted figures hurried out of the hotel bar. Others appeared quickly at windows or stepped from barns and sheds. Owlhoots all, they stared hard as the herd began to clatter past. Riding once more at the point, Stevens saw them. Erect and confident in the saddle, Pat gave the startled outlaws an impudent grin and a wink.

There was dynamite in this situation, as he knew only too well. His boldness alone held the outlaws motionless, puzzled and uncertain how to take this barefaced effrontery. The defiant yells and vigorous activity of Ezra and Sam farther along the flowing stream of steers and the determined absorption of Burnett filled the outlaws with further astonishment. Pat had counted on the paralyzing effect of this cool display, and for the moment at least he had guessed entirely right.

It would take some twenty minutes to ram the herd on through Tascosa and beyond, if they made it at all. Already, in the first few minutes, the time seemed to drag fatally. Stevens barely had time to entertain this grim thought when his hard gaze fixed on Lasher as the outlaw leader ran from the doorway of a store a hundred yards beyond the hotel.

Taking in the herd and reading its significance instantly, Blue Jaw glared wickedly at Pat. Two or three cronies who had followed him to the street stared in their turn. Notified by spies of Pat's presence on this range, they were startled by his brazen course in driving straight through Tascosa. The full significance of the drive eluded them until one of the owlhoots raked the lumbering steers with hard scrutiny.

"Look at that brand, Blue," he bawled above the rumbling uproar of the drive. "It's that Diamond L stuff, by grab—!"

Staring in disbelief, several outlaws abruptly guffawed their startled appreciation of the discovery. One slapped his knee and another threw up both hands.

"What keeps these wolves from jumping us, Sam?"

Burnett threw at him from behind in a tense undertone. Trinket, riding not far from Polk, also waited for the answer.

"They recognize this beef," Sam explained hurriedly. "It's the same stuff they stampeded, trying to scatter the roans. . . . Don't you savvy?" His voice dropped lower. "They think we *lifted* it!"

Polk was indigsant. "You mean they take *us* for rustlers? . . . Nonsense! Hang it all, Sam, they know better—"

"Don't fool yourself, boy," Sam's snaggle-toothed grin was shrewd. "A crook thinks every man is crooked, or he wouldn't be one himself. They figure we sure enough rustled this herd, all right, or we'd never have the gall to show ourselves here!"

Trinket looked awed as she suddenly comprehended Pat's subtle plan. "But won't that make it—all the worse?"

"Not a bit." Sam speedily disabused her. "In fact, the owlhoot code is all that protects us now. Only an out-and-out renegade would lay a finger on another owlhoot's rustled beef." His grin was wolfish. "Lasher's plumb stumped and he knows it—that's why he's so mad. Look at the thundering scowl on his ugly puss!"

They were drawing so close to the obviously frustrated outlaw that they were forced to drop their muttered exchange. Blue Jaw Lasher had watched Stevens ride calmly past with something like stupefaction. But as Pat came riding back along the line of plodding steers, all business and pretending to pay attention strictly to his work, the fuming leader could scarcely contain his fury.

"Damn your hide, Stevens! You can't wave this under my nose and get away with it," he bawled savagely.

Pat turned deliberately to face him. "You still around Lasher?" he clipped off tersely, loud enough to be heard by all. "Shove off—or I'll be forced to come back when I'm not so busy and yank *your* hide." The very moderation of his tone lent weight to the contemptuous threat.

With the remembrance of their last meeting seared into his brain, Lasher lost his head completely as Pat started to ride coolly on past without further ado. Cursing luridly, the outlaw whipped out his gun.

Wheeling his bronc in a flash, Pat's own weapon was out, poised and ready, pointed upward. On the instant, however, the two grim-faced outlaws nearest Lasher promptly grappled with him, restraining his murderous impulse by dint of strenuous effort. For several seconds the three men struggled, lurching this way and that in the roiling dust clouds that obscured their forms.

"Lay off it, Blue," rasped one of his friends condemningly. "We won't stand by and watch Stevens murdered because he's a sharper man and he's got you buffaloed. Take your medicine now!"

Lasher at length sensibly desisted, his strained face dark as a thundercloud. It may have been belated prudence that persuaded him to allow one of his men to relieve him of his gun. The outlaw gave vent to his feelings in further savage invective; but once Stevens made sure his teeth were drawn, he turned away indifferently.

His coolness in the face of deadly risk had its effect on the watching owlhoots. It seemed plain to them that he considered the passage through Tascosa no more than a routine chore. Any deepseated impulse to make trouble for him appeared to die on the spot, and they took out their admiring envy in ribald jibes hurled at the busy drovers.

"Working pretty hard for a few dollars, ain't you?" one of the outlaws taunted Ezra from the edge of a supply store porch. "Where's your helpers?"

Ez managed a surprised look. "Didn't you hear? Skurlock and his pals are all in the army by now. They weren't afraid to work toward what they wanted. What are you boys waiting for?"

His wily retort drew a curse or two. But in general

the outlaws accepted their defeat good-humoredly. Lasher watched the steers stream by for a few more minutes; then spinning violently on his heel he barged into the nearest saloon.

If he missed little that went on about him, Stevens seemed to have attention for nothing save the trampling herd. The steers drove on steadily, their dust fogging the street in thick ropes and clouds and driving the owlhoots to shelter. Polk and Trinket had passed on toward the point at an urgent signal from Pat and were already safely beyond the edge of town. Pat and Sloan rounded up the drag, hazing the last weary animals after the rest.

It seemed clear now that Pat's ruse had worked and there would be no immediate hitch in Tascosa. But neither he nor Sam relaxed their vigilance on that account. The picture could change in a flash as both well knew. All during the tense passage through town Stevens had watched uneasily for the appearance of Hook Larsen. A far tougher character than Lasher at bottom, violent and unpredictable in all he did, Hook was thoroughly capable of instigating a stampede at a moment's notice. But Larsen was nowhere to be seen.

Hazing the drag beyond the last buildings of town and making sure that Aunty Thankful brought the wagon in their wake without difficulty, Pat threw Sam a triumphant glance and wiped his grimy face with his damp kerchief. "So far so good," was his terse comment.

Sloan got his full meaning. He nodded. "We're not out of this yet," he qualified soberly. "Soon as them birds get to thinking this deal over they may change their minds about a few things. . . . No point in throwing a scare into that girl about it though," he added.

"No," Pat readily agreed. "But getting the stuff safe on her range is half the battle. We'll push right on to Saw Log and decide then what to do next."

The word went from one to another, and although Tascosa lay safely behind them now, they redoubled their efforts, urging the stock forward at a brisk pace.

Trinket Martin was faintly surprised by this display of energy. "Is it necessary to run them so close to home?" she called across to Pat.

"The sooner the quicker, Trink." He smiled disarmingly. "I don't trust that crowd in town either. Out of sight out of mind, you know—"

It satisfied her for the moment. But when the steers were turned out on Saw Log range an hour later and for the first time in days they felt at liberty to turn their attention to other things, Polk Burnett proved by his opening remark that he had been doing his own thinking.

"It worked there in town, Stevens—but maybe it wasn't so smart to give those outlaws the idea that this is rustled beef."

"How's that?" Pat drew him out, asking himself what was in the young man's mind.

"Not far enough from the Diamond L home range," Polk offered shortly. "Soon as Lasher learns you halted the stock here—and he will—he'll ask himself why. The only answer he can find spells grief for Trink Martin."

It was the same question Pat and Sam had been asking themselves. Surprised at the puncher's perspicacity, Pat had the fleeting thought that Burnett was maturing rapidly. "I know. . . . We'll just have to have our answer ready, boy."

"Yes?" Polk was skeptical. "What'll that be?" he pressed dryly.

Pat's grin was forced. "Oh, that'll depend on circumstances at the moment," he gave back.

Polk gave Trinket a sober look. "I sure hope you can figure out how to meet them. I'm taking it for granted, Stevens, that you'll see us through this and not rush off to Powder Valley in a sweat," he concluded pointedly.

It was in vain that Pat waited to learn whether the girl had caught Polk's slip of the tongue in using the plural pronoun. Apparently Trinket found nothing wrong with the statement; she only waited anxiously for Pat's reply.

"Oh, sure. We'll stick around for a day or two," Pat assured her carelessly. "I don't anticipate any serious trouble—but we'll keep a close watch out for spies anyway."

The men did not cease their labors at once. Watering in Cheyenne Creek, the stock spread out over the lush bottoms to graze and rest. At Pat's suggestion they were kept reasonably well bunched, so that they could be more easily guarded.

Aunty Thankful had driven the Saw Log wagon straight to the ranch house, and almost at once smoke curled upward from the chimney as she whipped together a makeshift supper. At Pat's insistence Trinket joined her. Later the faint clang of an iron triangle announced the meal. Sam and Polk rode in to eat while Stevens and Ezra watched the herd. Later they had their turn.

They were still at the house toward sunset when Burnett and Sloan raced in together to announce a rider sighted coming their way. "He's making straight for here, Stevens," said Sam significantly. "He's not even interested in that herd—"

Tightening up in a flash, the four men stepped out into the yard, and Trinket's worried gaze scanned the brush from the kitchen steps.

"There he comes." Polk grimly pointed out a tiny figure, black against the blood-red sweep of the sky.

"Could it be that he's—bringing some sort of an ultimatum from Lasher's gang?" the girl faltered.

"Hell, I'll fix that in a hurry," said Sam, starting to yank his worn carbine from the saddle-boot.

"No—hold on. We'll see who this is first," Pat warned sharply.

It was well that he did so. The rider advanced deliberately as they watched in taut silence. Five minutes later, peering sharply in the waning light, Ezra vented a gruff exclamation. "Shucks, that's no owlhoot," he declared. "Good thing we didn't try to scare *him* out with a shot or two. . . . It's Ed Roman, our old friend the federal marshal."

20

ALTHOUGH ROMAN was indeed an old acquaintance, he was far from a friend of the Powder Valley trio where the letter of the law was concerned. They had clashed with him before on minor points; but the officer was sternly just, and his presence here now promised a salutary effect on their fortunes.

"Howdy, Roman." Pat nodded with cool composure as the lawman jogged forward and drew rein.

Fully as tall as Ezra, and rawboned in the bargain, Roman flopped a big hand casually. He swept them all with a dour scrutiny. "What brings you to Tascosa, Stevens?"

"Delivering some Bar ES roans to the army at Matagorda," Pat supplied briefly, indication Sam and Ez. "On our way back we drove a beef herd Miss Martin picked up." He paused. "Little off the beaten track yourself, aren't you?"

The marshal shrugged. "It happens I'm tracing Hook Larsen, the owlhoot ringleader in that busted railroad riot up north—" He broke off as if waiting.

Pat's manner was still casual. "Know who you mean," he allowed. "Larsen was in this country when we went south. . . . We didn't spot him in Tascosa today as we came through, though." He looked up suddenly. "It might just pay you to scout around a while, Ed," he suggested.

Trinket and the others waited alertly for the other man's response. "I'll do that." Roman's gruff assent made no concession, however. "Anybody on the place who can give me any information?"

They explained that they had just arrived. Invited

to remain overnight by Trinket, and told he was welcome to make Saw Log his headquarters for as long as he wished, Roman gave little indication that he believed everything he was told. He ate supper stolidly by himself and found occasion later to query Polk Burnett in persistent detail; he even interrogated Aunty Thankful. She gave him scant satisfaction, vociferously stating her low opinion of Larsen and all his ilk.

It did not escape Roman that a close watch was kept on the beef herd overnight. Whatever conclusion he drew from this, he was one of the first up the following morning and soon rode off through the cottonwoods along Cheyenne Creek.

"We'll see him again. He'll be scouting around for a couple of days." Pat took prompt advantage of the opportunity thus offered. "Dig up your irons, Trink," he told the girl. "We'll slap the Saw Log brand on those Diamond L steers in a hurry."

Despite a protest over what he considered precipitate action, Polk pitched in with the others. Trinket herself was in the thick of the work, and midday saw the branding well under way. By evening a respectable number of cows were already under the Saw Log iron.

Though a vigilant watch was kept, no glimpse of spying outlaws was obtained; but Pat made it plain that he did not expect this state of affairs to continue for long. Roman failed to show show up for supper, and Polk expressed dismay that their legal protection, such as it was, should have faded away. The marshal returned at a late hour, however, and turned in at the barn as before.

When Burnett reconnoitered shortly after dawn the following morning, Roman was already gone. The puncher shook his head. "He won't be much good to us, busy as he is," he muttered to Stevens.

Pat shrugged. "This is nothing new for him. I'm just wondering how long it'll be before Lasher's crowd catches on that he's around."

Sam heard them talking. "You reckon they'll scatter when they hear it?" he asked.

Pat wasn't sure. "Roman's pretty close-mouthed about who else he's after besides Larsen. We can only hope."

No time was lost in turning once more to the branding. The beef had been allowed to scatter during the night for better feed, and Sam was busy chousing in the strays. Within an hour he was back at the branding corral with news.

"The wolves are gathering around, Stevens," the stocky man burst out portentously.

Polk looked around in surprise. "Nonsense! You won't see any lofers at this hour—" Ezra's grim chuckle awakened him to his mistake. His face went taut. "You mean Lasher's spies have shown up?"

"Nothing else. . . . Look, Stevens." Sam was all business. "I've been needing tobacco—" he began tentatively.

Pat's glance was comprehending. "All right, Sam." He was terse. "Get on into Tascosa, and get back here fast. Mind now, we'll be expecting you."

Needing no further urging, Sam promptly turned his pony and single-footed on his way. For a mile he clung to Cheyenne Creek and the cover of dense willows; then he turned and made straight for the Tascosa trail. No sign of activity met his gaze until, close to town, he saw a Mexican lad herding a handful of goats. If his nerves were strung tight and his beady black eyes were busy, he rode into Main Street with a show of casual indifference.

At first glance Tascosa appeared deserted. Two brawny men struggling with a balky horse in a corral farther down told Sam the truth. A man standing in a shed doorway ignored his offhand wave and continued to stare at him with bright hard eyes. Sam understood now that the outlaws were still here in full force.

His stubborn belief that he could bluff it out was not shaken when a sharp glance along the street showed him other men moving about. Kneeing his mount to a brisker pace, he made straight for the first general store.

He drew up before the place and was starting to swing down when a gun abruptly cracked from somewhere down the street. He felt a sharp tug at the brim of his battered hat. A harsh cry rang out. Hurrying figures came into sight, one pointing toward him.

Sam jerked out his Colt and fired over the heads of the group. One or two ducked behind a cottonwood trunk. More men were bursting out of store doors, and the town seemed suddenly full of hostile warriors.

Sam gave up then, hauling his mount around and urging it off the street into a brushy gap between buildings. More guns crashed, and the yelling was like the hunting call of a pack of wolves. He caught the pound of pursuing hoofs and gave himself wholly to the task of escaping.

It was easy for the first few minutes as he crashed away through the tall brush under the cottonwoods along the river bottom. As the cover thinned, however, guns again cracked viciously to the rear and twigs rained down from overhead. Sam sternly set himself to outdistance the determined owlhoots.

Reaching the open range, he set off at a headlong pace. The gunfire from behind sounded fainter, but looking back he saw at least a half dozen pounding riders. Apprehension clawed at his vitals. "Stevens won't thank me for leading this gang out to Saw Log," he grunted tensely. But no other sanctuary was offered on this prairie unless he took his chances of holing up in a buffalo wallow.

The renegades pressed him hard. They were gaining; their slugs whined overhead. Gazing anxiously beyond, Sam glimpsed the Saw Log corrals. He raced on to gain time to spread the warning. Pat and the others had been watching, however. They saw him flying forward, heard the firing, and were gathered at the branding corral, where posts and log supports offered some promise of protection, when he clattered up.

"Right inside here, Sam," ordered Stevens crisply. They swung the gate and clapped it shut after him. "Now, what's up out there—?"

Sam explained tersely. He had hardly ended before, half a dozen strong, the outlaws boldly advanced. Their guns had fallen silent, but clearly they meant to ride straight forward.

"Uh-oh." Polk was pale and grim. "That's Blue Jaw Lasher in the lead, Stevens. They mean business this time!"

"So do I." Pat was cold and stony. "Just leave this to me. . . . What are you after, Lasher?" He raised his voice as the outlaw leader pressed close.

Lasher led his confederates to within twenty yards of the corral, where they spread out. In no hurry, the big owlhoot glanced over the branding operation with a condemnatory look. "You're putting the Saw Log iron on this stuff, Stevens."

"What of it?" Pat's tone was bland. "It has to be done. Trink Martin's got her bill of sale from old Moze Lafey, all square and legal—if that concerns you."

Lasher went apopletic with rage. "What kind of a game is this?" he roared. "We thought you lifted that beef—"

Pat's retort was sharp. "Did you hear us *tell* anyone that?"

Stow the gab, Blue," an outlaw ripped out as Lasher began afresh. "These smart hombres are pulling a fast one here! Do we take over or not?"

They were well able to do so, with their advantage in numbers. Yet the Powder Valley men were equally determined to resist. The first click of a gun hammer would almost certainly precipitate swift carnage. Lasher glanced sharply about, gauging the position of his men.

"Open that gate, Sloan," he burst out harshly. "We're moving in—"

"Looking for work, are you?" A new voice cut in, hard and incisive. Momentarily frozen with surprise, the owlhoots glanced slowly around—to find Marshal Roman regarding them coldly from a strategic distance, a rifle slanted carelessly across his saddle-bow. "Well, speak up! What is going on here?"

A grim smile touched Pat's thin lips. "I'm not sure,

Roman. Maybe Lasher will explain," he suggested pointedly.

Blue Jaw struggled for words, his frustrated face a study. He knew Roman. "Never mind. It's nothing we can't settle without a crowd around," he managed finally. Roman waited grimly for more, but nothing came. With obvious reluctance the outlaw leader turned his horse, and his fellows followed suit. Not until they were beyond earshot and heading unmistakably toward Tascosa did the federal marshal speak.

"Got anything to say, Stevens?" he demanded.

"Me?" Pat's evasion was smooth. "You saw what I saw, Roman. Meanwhile we've got work waiting here. I don't know about you—but we'll be getting back to ours right now."

Roman watched for a time as they turned briskly back to the branding. Later he drifted away. They kept a strict watch, but there was no further disturbance that day and it seemed plain the outlaws had changed their minds about making immediate trouble.

The night proved equally peaceful, and the next morning saw the end of the task. Pat thought the steers, now under the Saw Log brand, would be safer if allowed to spread out naturally on the range. Trinket Martin's thanks was profuse and sincere. "I *must* get in to the bank and pay off Sam and Ezra's loan," she declared ruefully.

At Pat's query she explained that Dirk Morehouse, proprietor of the one big mercantile and supply house in Tascosa, ran a private bank in connection with his establishment. Polk Burnett's mirthless laugh was disillusioning.

"Do you think you can walk through Lasher's crowd with the cash price of a herd in your hand?" he asked pointedly. "I'm going with you, girl—"

Pat thought swiftly. "We'll all go," he decided. "Ed Roman seems to be prowling around somewhere as usual. No help from him. But the fact that he's not far off should tighten things up there in town long enough for our purpose."

The girl's strained face showed her relief. "You'll be more than welcome, Pat. We'll go immediately."

It was not long before all were ready. They set off for town in a group. Little was said on the way. Tascosa looked so deserted when they arrived that it had the air of an ominous trap. Pat led the way to an empty hitch-rack and they dismounted. Starting together up the sidewalk path toward Morehouse's adobe-walled store, they were spotted. A head withdrew from a window, and a man hastily stepped in off a porch.

Suddenly three men moved into sight, blocking their path. Blue Jaw was in the middle, his blazing eyes fixed immovably on Pat. "Stevens, you brought Ed Roman here," he lashed out, a taut nerve beating in his pale blue scar. "You'll settle now for a lot of things!"

Deadly menace hung in the heavy silence, as Pat's gaze held the owlhoots momentarily in check. Before more could be said, a ragged outbreak of cries and gunshots sounded from farther downstreet. Startled, all turned to look.

"That's Hook Larsen!" exclaimed Sam. "And Roman's three jumps behind him—"

With an abrupt scrape and scuttle of boots, Lasher and his confederates whipped around a corner into concealment; until this moment none of them had guessed at the federal marshal's presence in Tascosa. Polk cried out in dismay. *"Watch this, Stevens!"* he yelled warningly.

For answer, Pat sprang into the street. Pantherish and incredibly fast, Larsen was pelting toward him. The marshal called out harshly, firing over his head. Spotting Stevens, the burly outlaw turned, racing across the open street to plunge between buildings.

"Block him, Stevens," roared Roman. "The rest of you spread out and close in! He's making for the Canadian!"

Yells rang up and down the street and a Colt cracked from somewhere. But already the owlhoots were fleeing in numbers. Pat raced around the shed behind which Larsen had dived.

There was a flurry of firing as the two men almost collided at the rear. Pat felt a red-hot burn across his thigh, and Larsen's hat sailed away. Bellowing, Hook wheeled and fled back the way he had come.

A trio of hard-riding outlaws came pounding forward just as Larsen reached the street. "This way, Larsen!" they bawled, reining down. Seeking possible escape, the outlaw leader sprang out and sought to swing astride behind one of them. He nearly made it. But at that moment Pat shot out from the alley, launching himself in a flying dive, and brought his quarry down in the dust with a thump.

Roman unleashed a throaty blast, and the other renegades raced on. *"Stevens, look out!"* Burnett's yell knifed the tension. Roughly subduing Larsen, Pat did not even look back. A double crash of guns immediately behind him smote his ears. He was in time to see Lasher collapse sprawling in a final contortion, with Burnett striding out to stand over him, his smoking gun still ready.

"Polk!" Trinket Martin's clear voice rang vibrantly in the suddenly returned silence. She rushed out, throwing herself on him in a fever of apprehension. "Are you all right? You're not hit—?"

"Well now," Roman's heavy tone rumbled as he helped haul Larsen erect, a glowering captive, "it's not every day a lucky puncher can save Stevens' life and pick up a chunk of reward money at the same time. I saw you bag Lasher before I could make a move," he vouchsafed gruffly, nodding to Polk in complete approval.

"He did even better, Roman," interposed Sam, coming forward with Ezra. "From here, I'd say he got himself a permanent job with a ranch we been working for—"

"That's right," pursued Ez sagely. "Saw Log needs a man's hand, quiet as it'll be around here from now on."

Trinket turned within the protective circle of Polk's sinewy arm, rosy but unabashed. "You've both been plotting this," she accused them roguishly. "I saw it right from the first. Bless your hearts, I'm not the least bit sorry you've won!"

"Oh well—" Ezra shook his grizzled head piously. "A man's got to look after these reckless youngsters, like it or not. . . . I move the ceremony be pushed ahead—say to this afternoon—so a couple of old stagers like Sam and me can push on home to Powder Valley and get our rest."

"And another thing," urged Sam with mock earnestness. "With money coming, right now we can afford a wedding present. Likely we couldn't, once Ez gets tangled up in the next poker game we run across."

Ezra slashed at him with his hat in pretended fury, and Sam's surprisingly agile footwork evoked the lighthearted laughter of them all.